DE'LURE PUBLICATIONS

De'Lure Shorts & Poems

TEN ORIGINAL SHORT STORIES & POEMS

De'Lure Shorts

& Poems

De'Lure

My Personal Investors

To my personal Investors, I love you all very, very much. Your love and belief in my talent will live inside of my books and my heart for eternity and for that I am so grateful. Thank you all for going out of your way to invest in my dream in many different ways.

Edna Rowell AL
Valerie Olivier NY
Carol Burton AL
Brandilyn Hayes AL
Britney Latrice AL
James Bryant OK
Lamar Jones AL
Alexus Calvin AL
Pashale Calhoun AL
Rita Lowry AL
Quana Lane AL
Paige Marie NY
Terrilynn Dunning AL
Ravon McDade AL
Chantay Calhoun AL
Martenia Shyne IL
Cheryl Cece Curry AZ
Charita Calhoun AL
Kela King AL
Samantha Blackmon FL
Regina Kennedy AL
Brittany Williams AL
Jordan Lee Aune MN

Welcome all to De'Lure Shorts & Poems. The ten mind-blowingly realistic short stories you'll read in this book will all be later released as either full length novels or Movies. As always my stories are all born from pure imagination, and are written to seem, and feel real but are not to be perceived as such. This is beautiful, gripping, unforgettable fiction... but it is still fiction nonetheless.

I Will

"Marcus, where the hell are we going?" Alexandria asks.

He displays a smile on his handsome face but doesn't respond.

"Boy, I know you hear me talking to you." she nudges him playfully with her left elbow.

"Alex, can I just drive please..." Marcus wipes his brow.

"Hell no," Alex replies, "I know you Marcus, something's wrong... or maybe something's right. I don't really know, but you're trying to figure out a way to tell me something."

"Is that right?" Marcus never takes his eyes off the road ahead of him.

"That's exactly right," Alex assures him, "Whenever something is going on with you, you get that nervous look on your face that you have right now."

"What nervous look?" Marcus looks over at her.

"That one," she points at his smooth dark face, "You've been making that face since elementary school."

"Damn," Marcus smirks, "I don't have a clue what you're

talking about, but somebody's been watching me mighty damn close."

"Don't flatter yourself," Alex looks away, "Ain't nobody watching yo goofy ass. And I'm referring to Valentine's Day... fifth grade... the pink teddy bear..."

"Damn," Marcus bursts into reminiscent laughter, "Girl I had the biggest crush in the world on you back then."

"Yeah I know." Alex replies.

"You were so short," Marcus stares back at the road, "pretty yellow skin and your hair was so long and dark. Perfect eyes, a beautiful smile, and that voice... oh my God Alex, even back then you had the voice of a godangel." Alex laughs.

"Marcus, what the hell is a godangel?" she asks.

"Hell, I don't know," he replies, "But that's exactly what you sounded like when you sang."

Alex turns towards the window to hide her reddening cheeks from him.

"And yeah, I remember that Valentine's day," Marcus tells her, "Damn, Alex that was fifteen years ago today. We've been best friends ever since that day."

"Damn, today is Valentine's Day huh?" Alex asks. Marcus laughs.

"You need a man Alex," he tells her, "what female forgets about Valentine's Day?"

"A single one like me." she replies with no hesitation.

"It's all good," Marcus says, "You don't really need a man anyway, you got me. You know you finally fell in love with me our senior year in high school..."

"Boy please," Alex says, "That was a long time ago, you were cute back then."

"Right," Marcus says with that charming smile that she can't resist, "that was a looong time ago."

2

De'Lure

The deafening awkward silence is killing Alexandria.

"So," she says, "What's going on with that freak you were dating a while back?"

"You mean my girlfriend of two years," Marcus asks with a smile, "She's good, we're good... you know, everything is good right now."

"Good," Alex says, "I'm glad you're happy. One question though, if you're so happy with her why do you spend so much time around me?"

"Who else would I spend my time around?" he asks.

"Um, your girlfriend..." Alex tells him.

"Right," he replies, "But I mean beyond that..."

Alex laughs awkwardly.

"What do you mean beyond that Marcus," Alex asks, "There is no beyond that. Love is love, and it should be absolute or not at all."

Marcus smiles at her.

"I agree," he says through pure white teeth, "And what Steve Harvey book did you steal that from?"

"No sir," she replies, "You know I don't do Steve I only read De'Lure. But I'm glad you agree with the fact that love should be absolute. So with that said, answer my question."

"What was the question again," Marcus asks, "I'm sorry I forgot just that fast."

"If you have been with her for two years," Alex wets her lips, "Why do you not go a day without seeing me?"

"Seriously Alex," Marcus says, "You're my best and only friend. You know I can't function without you baby."

"Don't do that." Alex says.

"Don't do what, baby?" Marcus inquires.

"That," she frowns, "Never call me baby. I'm not your baby, I'm your friend. And by the way, your girlfriend should be your best female friend."

"Well, in any event," Marcus starts, "I'm glad you took off work today to be with me on this special day."

"No sir," Alex says, "I did not take off work. You came in my job and told my boss there was an emergency, and we've been driving ever since. Now we're stopping. Why are we stopping here at Dansby's?"

"It's a jewelry store." Marcus tells her.

"I know what it is Marcus," Alex replies, "But why did you bring me, your single friend to a jewelry store on Valentine's Day? Do you have any idea how cruel that is?"

"Not today Alex," he says, "This is important, please don't get all emotional on me, not today."

Alex exhales deeply as she crosses her arms over her chest.

"Fine Marcus." she fakes a smile.

"Thank you," he flashes that smile again, "Now come on I need your help."

He reaches over and unfastens her seatbelt. Then he steps out of his car and walks around to the passenger door.

Alexandria is still staring straight ahead with a million thoughts swirling through her crowded brain. She's not stupid, she knows full well what Marcus needs help with at a jewelry store on Valentine's Day. He opens her door and waits for her to step out. Side by side the two enter the jewelry store.

"Well aren't you two a gorgeous couple," a thin white employee says as they approach one of the jewelry cases. "Welcome to Dansby's. My name is Evelyn what can I show you two today?" she asks.

"Oh no, we're just friends." Alex says quickly.

"Oh... okay," Evelyn replies, "I'm sorry. Well in any event how can I help you both today?"

Marcus smiles down at his uncomfortable friend.

"Show me the rings please." he says to the nice lady.

4

"Okay rings," Evelyn says, "Now are you looking for like a promise ring, a ring for mom…"

"No ma'am," Marcus replies, "Show me the **engagement** rings please."

Alexandria's heart stops cold. She can't feel her face, and as she looks up into Marcus' eyes the warm feeling his gaze usually gives her is gone.

"Engagement…" Alex whispers following closely behind Marcus and Evelyn.

"Yeah it's a surprise," he says turning around to smile at her, "and I want you to pick the ring out for me."

Even though there are no tears on her face Alexandria is definitely crying on the inside. She's been single for five years now because secretly she's been waiting for Marcus to realize how perfect she could be for him. But apparently he still hasn't and never will. In her mind as long as he wasn't married there was still hope that he could love her. But no, today all those hopes and dreams come to an end.

"Here we are sir," Evelyn says, "What kind of ring did you have in mind for your special lady?"

"Well I don't really know," Marcus stares back at a stone-faced Alexandria.

"Come here Alex." He prods.

She steps up beside him closer to the rings. Staring down at the rows, and rows of gorgeous rings that she'll probably never own herself, Alex continues to fight her building emotions.

"Alex…" Marcus says.

"What Marcus?" she replies blankly; her yellow face is turning red by the second.

"If you were my girl," he starts, "Which one of these rings would literally take your breath away, forcing you to say I do…"

"I don't want to…" Alex mumbles.

"Damn it Alex, please just choose." Marcus prods.

She exhales deeply.

"Marcus," Alex takes another step forward wiping a tear from her left eye, "If I… was your girl, I would be happy with whatever ring you decided to give me. But… love and engagements are important memories that every girl should cherish forever, so… I say get her that chocolate diamond ring in the back set in rose gold."

"Are you sure Alex?" Marcus asks.

She looks up into his clueless eyes again wishing and praying he could just see her.

"Yes, Marcus I'm sure." she tells him.

"Thanks Alex," he bends down to kiss her warm cheek, "Ring it up please Evelyn."

Marcus hands Evelyn his credit card as Alex heads towards the door.

"But sir don't you want to know the price?" Evelyn asks.

"No ma'am my money is good," he tells her, "And my girl's worth every penny and a billion more."

Evelyn swipes his card.

"Alex…" Marcus says, as she pushes the heavy glass door open to exit the store. She turns to look at him.

He walks towards her.

"You know," he says, "A wise young woman once told me that a man's girlfriend should be his best female friend, but I disagree."

"Yeah, I know you do." Alex replies turning to leave again.

"I think a man's best female friend should be his wife…" Marcus drops down on one knee as he opens the ring box.

"Alexandria LaDawn Taylor," Marcus looks deep in her soul, "Will you marry me…"

Alex looks past him at Evelyn whose tears are almost as plentiful as hers.

Evelyn's hands are up near her elated face pressed tightly together as she nods her head up and down to Alex.

Alex looks down into Marcus' chestnut eyes and can't seem to remember one word of the English language. This is a problem because English is the only language she's ever spoken.

"Alex…" Marcus stays put on his numbing knee.

"Yes…" she cries.

"Um, what do you think love?" he caresses her right hand in his.

"I think," she wipes away new tears, "This is the most… cruel thing any man has ever done to any woman."

Marcus lets her hand go and wrinkles his dark brows.

"But, I will say this," Alex cries, "That girl, your woman is the luckiest girl on the planet today and she doesn't even know it yet."

"Alex I…" Marcus reaches for her hand again.

She snatches away.

"No Marcus," she opens the door, "You do not use me to practice proposing to her! It's cruel and inconsiderate; I'll be in the car."

Marcus approaches Evelyn to retrieve his receipt as they look at each other they strangely understand the confusion on each other's' faces. Marcus takes his receipt and place the ring box the bag before heading out of the store.

As he approaches his car he bypasses the driver's side and makes his way to Alex's door. She looks up at him through the window red face and all awaiting his next rude move for the day.

Marcus attempts to open the door. It's locked. He knocks gently; then she unlocks the door and turns her head away from him.

Marcus calmly sits the ring bag down on the hood of the

car. He surveys his surroundings carefully, as he flexes his strong back.

Then he opens her door and without a word he snatches her out of the car and lifts her up just high enough in the air to sit her on top of his luxury car.

"Marcus what the hell..." Alex panics looking all around for help.

"Shut up," he growls, "Now I don't know what the hell your problem is woman, but you just made a complete fool out of me in that store. You were rude and obnoxious and I didn't appreciate your words at all."

"Marcus you..." she cries into his eyes.

"Alexandria," he growls, "*Shut up*! I was very nervous and skeptical about today... but I knew that once I had the perfect ring in hand and was down in position on one knee looking into those deep brown soulful eyes... I knew that was going to give me the courage to ask you. And it did..."

"Marcus, you didn't mean it..." she interjects.

"Woman, are you out of your rabbit ass mind?" he steps forward in between her open legs to look deeper into her eyes.

"I meant every single word I said to you in there," he swears, "And you with your sensitive attitude, trust issues, and smart ass mouth... you ruined it. You ruined everything. You look at your past and the idiots you chose to date while ignoring my ass all those many years and now you equate all men with those assholes."

"Lies..." she cries.

"Really Alex..." he reaches inside his front left pocket to retrieve his phone. He quickly hands his phone to her.

"What am I supposed to do with this," she asks, "and it's locked anyway."

"The code is your birthday and month." Marcus reveals.

Alex tries the code in disbelief. It works.

"Now what...?" she wipes more tears away.

"Go to my calendar," he instructs her, "and then tell me, what was the only thing I had planned to do today?"

She quickly finds and opens the calendar on his smart phone.

"Propose to Alex..." she whispers almost in a daze.

"I can't hear you Alex..." he yells turning around hoping there are people watching their exchange. To his surprise he has drawn quite a nice crowd behind him in the parking lot. He looks back into her searching eyes.

"Marcus..." Alex scoots towards him on top of the car.

"I'm not those guys from your past Alex," he vows, "I never have been. I've always been faithful, but I've just never been with the right girl."

"I want to love you Marcus..." she cries.

"You know what," he says looking up into her soul, "that night at Kelley Johnson's house; 11th grade year, in the basement... you remember that?"

"Like yesterday." Alex smiles down at him through her warm salty tears.

"You kissed me." Marcus recollects.

"We did more than kiss sir," she reminds him, "seems you're the one who's having trouble remembering that night."

"How could I ever forget," he puts a gentle hand on each one of her knees, "you see, that was just another wild night to you... but for me it was my very first time."

"Are you serious?" Alex gasps with both hands covering her slightly lipstick smeared mouth.

"Alex you were my first," he admits, "and honestly even though it only happened one time and it didn't last very long, that feeling I had with you that night was one I knew I could never recreate with any other girl or woman in my life."

"What are you saying Marcus..." Alex cries.

"I'm saying," he hesitates, "Alex, I'm twenty-seven years old now, and you're still the only woman I've ever been with… and that's okay, because I wanna die that way my love."

"Marcus don't say that…" Alex holds her breath as he picks her up off the top off the car and swings her around back down to the ground.

Marcus reaches inside the bag on the hood of his car. He slowly makes his way back down to his knee again.

"Now let's try this again," he opens the box and places the ring on her finger, "Alexandria LaDawn Taylor, I've loved you since hello. Now we missed each other's love many times over the years as we matured, but now that we are both grown, and of stable minds… I think we would both be foolish to not live out the rest of our days as man and wife. I'll love you until my casket drops girl, and even then I want you to continue to wear this ring and know that your heart will always, always, always belong to me."

"I WILL"

THE BEST PROPOSAL
IS ONE SHE'S NOT EXPECTING
WHEN HE RANDOMLY LAYS DOWN
HIS LOVE AND EXPRESSES
ALL THE WAYS HE ADORES AND NEEDS HER
AS HE VOWS THAT HIS LIFE'S MISSION
IS TO ALWAYS ADORE PLEASE HER
AS HE WAITS DOWN ON ONE KNEE
THE TEARS IN HER LONGING EYES
ARE ALL HE NEEDS TO SEE
NOW WITHOUT HESITATION
HE POPS THE QUESTION

De'Lure

THEN AS HER EYES AND LIPS SAY YES
HE ROARS TO HIS FEET BLESSING
HER WITH DELICATE KISSES
FROM HER LIPS TO HER CHEEK
HER SOUL IS ALL EARS
AS HIS HEART DOTH SPEAK
A NEW BOND IS FORMED
A MOMENT IN TIME IS SEALED
THERE'S NO GREATER JOY
THAN TRUE LOVE REVEALED

Sugar Coated

In a large house at the end of Sycamore drive in Orlando Florida, eighteen year-old Allison Whitehead is all alone in her bathroom. After she glumly flushes the toilet, she quickly snatches the plastic bag out of her small pink trashcan.

With the almost empty plastic bag clutched tightly in her right hand, she stares at the girl in the mirror. In her reflection Allison sees everything that everyone else wants her to be. It's so hard to be perfect, but that's what she is. She must be; she's been told so her entire life.

None of her family members or so-called friends have a clue about her private talks with herself and the screaming insecurities she has lived with for more years than she cares to remember. The standard that her father set in place for her is unreachable.

Ronald Whitehead, Allison's father, is the most successful

criminal defense attorney in the state of Florida. Most people hate the fact that he has freed over twenty terrifyingly dangerous serial criminals, but everyone respects his success rate and wealth due to that fact.

Allison's father is even more perfect than he's tried to force her to be. But Ally can't think or worry about her father right now, because she's got so many other things to stress over. Prom is coming up, graduation is around the corner, and letters of acceptance from college all over the country are covering her bedroom floor.

Most importantly her boyfriend Trey Elliston is supposed to be on his way to her house to surprise her. Ally has no idea what his surprise for her could be, but she has a surprise for him as well.

"Ally what are you doing in there," a voice asks from the other side of the bathroom door, "We've been downstairs waiting for you for half an hour."

Ally opens the door. "Cassidy, Kinsey, what are you two doing here?" Ally asks.

"It's Friday Ally," Kinsey says, "Did you forget you invited us over for a sleepover?"

"Oh no," Ally replies, "Was that supposed to be tonight?"

"Um duh," Cassidy bursts into obnoxious laughter, "Why, did you make other plans girl...?"

"No," Ally says, "Well yes... kinda. I don't know, never mind."

"Okay," Kinsey says, "Oh by the way Trey is downstairs."

"You bitch," Ally says nervously, "How long has he been down there?"

"Um we don't know Ally," Cassidy tells her, "he was here when we got here. But first things first, you need to go throw on some make up and run a comb through that blonde mess you call hair."

"Oh shut up Cassidy," Ally says playfully, "I still look better than you two hags."

Cassidy and Kinsey both gasp, then the three of them all begin laughing together.

"Okay I'm going to go fix myself up," Ally hands Kinsey the plastic bag from the bathroom, "Kinsey go throw this in the big trashcan outside. This is very important Kinsey please make sure you throw it away outside."

"Okay, okay," Kinsey replies, "God what's in here? Used condoms that you're hiding from your dad?"

"Of course not," Cassidy snatches the bag from Kinsey, "Everybody knows Allison Whitehead is the last known virgin on planet Earth."

"Cassidy, do not open that bag," Ally reaches out to grab it from her nosey friend, "Just let Kinsey go throw it away."

"Well I would have," Cassidy takes a few steps back, "But now you got me intrigued love and I wanna know your secret." Cassidy is having obvious trouble untying the knot in the top of the bag. In a sudden fit of frustration, the young mixed girl rips the bag open. "Cassidy

no!" Ally screams.

As soon as it hits the floor amongst the other assorted clutter Ally's two friends know exactly what it is, and what it means.

"Wait," Kinsey picks it up off the floor, "Are you kidding me Allison?"

"Oh... My... God," Cassidy snatches it from her red headed friend, "This is not real. This can't be, not little miss perfect. Oh my God, Allison..."

"Both of you in my room now..." Ally demands.

As the three of them enter Allison's huge bedroom, she quickly snatches her property out of her friend's hand and breaks it in half stuffing the debris in her sweat pants pocket.

Now sitting in front of her bedroom mirror, Ally looks past her reflection into the curious eyes of her two best friends in the world.

"Kinsey, come comb my hair please," Ally breaks the awkward silence, "and Cassidy, go in my closet and pick something cute for me to wear downstairs."

"What, like a burial dress?" Cassidy walks towards the huge walk-in closet.

"Oh shut up, Cassidy," Allison says, as Kinsey begins to comb her long pretty blonde hair. "My parents don't have a clue, and if they did they wouldn't be that angry. Well they would, but they won't ever find out so it really doesn't matter."

"It wasn't your mom and dad I was worried about." Cassidy says as she peeks her head back out of the closet, "If this gets out do you know what this would do to Trey's image and his future. He's the only kid in the country who's going to graduate this year as an All-American quarterback and class Valedictorian. The kid is projected to be an NFL superstar *and* an even better lawyer than your dad."

"Did you find me an outfit, or not, Cassidy?" Allison ignores her friend's dramatic spiel.

"Yep," Cassidy walks towards her, "I found two dresses. Which one do you prefer "graveyard gray", or "tombstone teal"?"

"Give me the blue dress Cassidy and sit down and shut up." Allison snatches the dress from her.

"I'm only kidding Ally," Cassidy says in an obviously apologetic tone, "I know how much Trey loves you, and I'm sure he won't leave you or judge you because of your mistake."

"Yeah thanks," Ally frowns, "How about the two of you go down there and send Trey up here."

"Fine..." Cassidy heads out of the door.

"Ally," Kinsey says, still combing her friend's hair, "No matter what I'm never gonna leave you. I love you and this doesn't change anything. You're still Miss Perfect to me."

"But I'm not, Kinsey," Ally says, "I never was. Nobody is perfect and now you both know I'm far from it, and soon Trey will know too. Just go get him please."

"Okay," Kinsey hands the comb to Ally, "Text me if you want me to come back up here and be with you."

"I'll be fine," Ally pulls her dress down over her head, "Thanks for understanding Kinsey."

"That's what best friends are for Ally," she replies, "Um, and don't forget to take those fugly sweat pants off, they do not go with that dress."

Kinsey smiles at Ally as she walks out closing the door behind her.

Back in front of her mirror all alone again Ally looks deep into her own green eyes. She's always heard that the eyes are the windows to a person's soul. She wishes now more than ever she could see her own soul.

Finally, there's a knock at the door. "Come in." Ally says.

The door opens.

"Tell me," the tall muscular teen phenom says, "How is it possible that you get even more beautiful *every* single time I lay eyes on you?"

Ally blushes.

"You really are Miss Perfect aren't you...?" Trey smiles.

"Ugh," Ally groans, "There's that word again. Nobody is perfect Trey... *especially* not me..."

"Shut up and get over here and kiss me." Trey interjects.

Allison does as she's told. While Trey kisses her like it's the very first time, the much shorter Ally stands on the   tips of her toes to run her fingers through the soft auburn curls of his hair.

After the kiss is over, Trey doesn't seem to want to let go.

"You are Miss Perfect." he whispers into her ear.

"No I'm not Trey," she replies, "Nobody is perfect."

"I know nobody is perfect," Trey holds her back so he can look into her calm emerald eyes, "But you are... You're perfect for me. You complete me and you make my life worth living."

She smiles.

"Said the rich, handsome, All-American quarterback slash Valedictorian. No, I'm pretty sure you're complete *with* or *without* me." Ally says blushing a little more.

"I brought you something." he tells her.

"Yeah I heard..." Ally replies with wide eyes.

"I know we're still very young," Trey starts, "and we haven't even really lived yet... and I mean I guess I don't even really know what life is. But whatever life is I wanna spend every second of the rest of mine with you."

Trey drops down on one sturdy knee before his gorgeous girlfriend. Out of his pocket he pulls a glistening ring.

"This is the ring my father used to propose to my mother," he tells her, "And now I'm giving it to you. Will you marry me Allison?"

As Trey looks up into her eyes her tears are all the confirmation he needs.

"I can't." she says.

"Awesome," he says, "Wait what do you mean you can't baby? You have to. You're a part of me... you're a part of my story and my American dream. You have to marry me."

"That's more important to you than anything Trey," she tells him, "You might love me, but you're in love with your image."

"So you don't want to marry me Allison?" Trey stands up.

"I want to," she replies, "But first I have a confession."

"About what?" he asks.

"Sit down on my bed." Allison points.

He obeys.

"Well," she looks down at her feet, "There is no easy way to say this and I wouldn't even know how to begin to sugar coat it so…"

"Damn it Ally just say it!" Trey demands.

"I'm pregnant." she blurts out with both eyes closed tightly.

Trey stands up as he bursts into forced laughter.

"That's cute baby," he says, "now do you have a real confession or you just feel like messing with me?"

Ally doesn't respond.

"You're joking right," he says, "See because you have to be joking… because you and I are both virgins so it's physically impossible for you to be pregnant… Right baby?"

Allison continues to cry.

"How did you get pregnant Ally?" he asks.

"It wasn't supposed to happen," she cries, "He… came home *really* drunk one night about a month ago…"

"He," Trey yells, "He who!"

"My dad," she cries, "My mom was at the grocery store and he and I were here alone. He wanted to, and I just wanted him to be happy. And then I missed my period and I just took a test today… And…"

Out of her pocket Allison pulls the two broken pieces of the pregnancy test she took earlier and hands them to Trey. He looks at it and then quickly throws it to the floor.

"It's true," he says, "So now everybody's gonna know…"

"No," she interjects, "Nobody can know anything. I'll take care of it."

Trey heads towards the door in a rage.

18

"Trey, don't leave me…" she cries as she falls to her knees, "baby please don't leave me."

"You let him ruin my life," Trey says, "Do you have any idea how embarrassing this is for me? If the newspapers got wind of this sick twisted shit, my image would be destroyed Allison! Do not leave this room, I'm gonna take care of this."

As he closes the door behind him Allison rushes to her closet to hide. She prays as she listens for the altercation that's she's sure is about to take place between Trey and her father.

BANG BANG. Ally hears two loud gunshots.

BANG BANG BANG. Three more shots ring out from downstairs.

Her door opens but she doesn't hear anything else. She can hear her heart pounding loudly in her ears.

"Daddy…" she cries.

"You wish," Trey says from somewhere nearby, "Come here Allison."

"Trey what did you do?" she asks, through her warm tears. "Something I should have done a long time ago," he replies, "I got rid of all the poisonous people in your life. Now we can go get you an abortion, claim that what happened here was self-defense and move on with our lives together. You'll get everything your father left you in his will and we'll have a long wonderful life together."

"Kinsey and Cassidy…" Allison cries walking out of the closet.

"Kinsey is fine," Trey says, "I had to get rid of Cassidy though I never liked her."

"My mom…" Ally cries.

"She's gone," Kinsey cries, entering the room shaking uncontrollably, "Everybody is gone now… I guess it was for the best though. Trey, told me what your dad did to you, it's really sick Ally. Whatever you want me to tell the police I will. I told you no matter what, I'll never leave you."

"What the hell, Trey?" Ally screams.

"Everything will be fine Allison…" Kinsey rubs her best friends back.

"Are you crazy Kinsey," Ally grabs the red head by her slender face, "This is not going to be fine!"

"And you…" Ally turns around to find the barrel of Trey's gun pointing directly between her eyes.

"SUGAR COATED"

WHEN YOU LOOK IN THE MIRROR
DOES THE TRUTH STARE BACK AT YOU
OR DO YOU DENY THE REFLECTION
BEYOND THE MAGNITUDE OF WHAT THAT COULD DO
ALL THE EVIL WHISPERING VOICES
WHIRLING IN AND OUT OF YOUR MIND
YOU NEVER CAN CRY ENOUGH TEARS
TO RENDER YOURSELF BLIND
BUT THAT'S FINE BECAUSE WHAT YOU FIND
IN THAT GLASS SHRINE IS BY DESIGN
LEARN TO ADORE YOU
OR YOU'LL NEVER KNOW A LOVE OUTSIDE YOUR
OWN MIND

The Littlest Country Star

The summer is definitely here now and the sun is out every day with a vengeance. And every night, just like tonight the sweet Alabama air is filled with butterflies and mosquitoes.

School's out, so all the local malls and parks in every city in Alabama are bursting with kids of all ages and backgrounds pretending to be something they're not. But, they're kids and that's what you do, put on a front that you're better than the next person to hide the insecurities inside yourself.

On the interstate somewhere near Auburn, Alabama there's a lime green 2005 Volkswagen Beetle going about eighty miles an hour headed towards a familiar city. A young mother and her much younger son are running back home from the big bad real world again. She's five feet tall with the body of a Hooter's waitress and the mind of a McDonald's fry cook.

Her strawberry blonde hair is falling all around her almost gorgeous face in unraveling curls. Her baby blue eyes are set on the short road ahead to a house she said she would never set foot in again.

As she looks down at her adorable six-year-old son Taylor, she remembers all the dreams she had before he ever came into her life. She doesn't regret him, but she does know that his existence ended her hopes for a better lifestyle. His short cropped hair is the same strawberry blonde tint as hers, but he has his daddy's eyes. She would die right now for that boy to live forever.

Hi, my name is Tonya Little and I'm twenty-nine years old. My son Taylor is my whole world, or at least what's left of it. We were doing okay, but I lost both of my jobs so we gotta do what we gotta do. God, be with us.

Alabama, Montgomery, Alabama to be exact, is a city filled with broken dreams. Like most towns, Montgomery is filled with all kinds of people, good and bad. It's not the worst place on earth, but I can't understand for the life of me why anybody would ever come or wanna live here. Alabama is a retirement state, so if you're old and withered and you've already given up on hopes and dreams this place is suitable for you. But, if you really wanna be somebody in this world, this is not the place for you.

I had a dream once. Connor, my ex-boyfriend and Taylor's dad, is a traveling country singer. I started out as one of his backup singers, and I thought if I just kept singing with him, just maybe, one day I could get a record deal of my own. The truth is I'm just not as good as Connor is, and I never will be.

"Mommy..." Taylor says.

"Yes Pumpkin." Tonya replies.

"Tell me the story again mama." he looks up at her with wide steel gray eyes.

Tonya smiles down at her handsome son, and knows she would never deny him a thing in this world.

"Look up at the sky baby," she tells him, "do you see the North star?"

"Uh huh…" Taylor says.

"When I was a little girl," his mother continues, "I never wanted to be at home. So, I used to get lost a lot, and your grandfather Willy would always have to come find me. So one day, he told me that I was the wandering type, and that I was probably going to be running away from home for a very long time. So he looked way up in the sky and showed me the North Star, for the first time. But, he didn't call it the North Star he called it the country star. He told me that any time I got lost at night I could look up into the sky, and follow the country star all the way back home again. And you know what?"

"What mommy?" Taylor asks.

"Your grandfather was right," she admits, "I've been running away ever since. But, for some reason, I always end up following that star right back home again."

Two hours later, they pull up to a nice house, in a decent neighborhood, in Montgomery Alabama. Tonya inhales deeply, and then exhales slowly. Then she looks down at Taylor and smiles.

"You ready son?" Tonya asks.

"I was born ready mama." he returns her contagious smile.

As the two of them make their way up the dark steps to the front door, Taylor, who is just a couple of steps behind his mother is running his left hand up the wooden rail. Tonya rings the doorbell several times.

"Coming…" a sweet, but tired voice says from the inside. "Ouch!" Taylor yelps in the darkness.

Tonya looks back at him as the front door opens.

"Tonya…" the woman at the front door says to the back of her head.

"What's wrong, Taylor?" Tonya makes her way back down the stairs towards him.

"My finger, mommy." he tells her.

"Taylor, baby let me see..." the woman from the front door approaches them.

"He's my son, mom," Tonya pulls the boy away from her; "I can take care of him."

"If that's the case," a strong voice says from the doorway, "What the hell are you doing back here?"

"Nice to see you too, Dad..." Tonya looks up at the tall graying man.

Without another word he makes his way down the steps, picks up the crying six-year-old, and carries him back inside the house.

Once inside the house, he sits the boy down in a chair at the kitchen table. As Tonya and her mother look on from the doorway of the kitchen, her father grabs a small needle from a nearby drawer.

With a stern look on his face, he makes his way back to his young grandson.

"Well now, son," he says as he takes Taylor's shaking hand in his much larger hand, "I know it's been a couple of years, but you still remember your old grandpa don't you?"

Taylor nods his head up and down, and his grandfather smiles.

"I broke my hand, grandpa." Taylor explains though the tears.

"Well now you didn't break it," grandpa says, "but you did pick up a nasty splinter. But it's out now and your finger's as good as new."

"Thanks grandpa." Taylor smiles, wiping old tears away.

"Well now, that's what grandpas are for, right?" he says , "now dry those tears away son, you're almost a grown man, now."

"Grandpa," Taylor flashes an adorable little grin, "I'm only six years old."

De'Lure

"It's never too early to start becoming a man Taylor," his grandfather returns his smile as he kneels down to kiss the boy on top of his head, "one day your mama's gonna get old like me and you'll have to look after her."

Grandpa Willy looks over at his daughter, and she knows exactly what that look means.

"Everything is fine dad," Tonya says, "we were just passing through and decided to stop by."

"At one o'clock in the morning Tonya?" Grandpa Willy asks, "Doesn't sound like just passing through to me. You know, your mother and I fell asleep on the couch in the den. If we had been in bed you would have been stuck out here all night with my crying grandson. Tell me, did you ever get in touch with that ex-boyfriend yours again? I saw him on TV the other day at some country music awards show."

"No," Tonya walks towards her son, "and dad if you're just gonna keep throwing that in my face we'll just leave!"

"Oh... please don't leave yet," her father says, "you haven't even raided my refrigerator or stolen any money yet."

"Not in front of my son," Tonya says, "I do not steal dad, and we don't need your food!"

Grandpa Willy looks down at Taylor with knowing eyes.

"Are you hungry, son?" Grandpa asks.

Taylor hesitates and then nods his head up and down.

"Linda," grandpa Willy says, "fix the boy and his mama some grits, eggs, and sausage. I know she's starving too, even though she won't admit it."

"Whatever," Tonya says, "I don't steal, dad."

"You're right," her father says, "you never have been good at getting away with anything. The only thing you're good at is running away. Tonya, I can't remember the last time you stayed here longer than 48 hours."

Taylor looks up at his mom. As she looks back down at him she doesn't have a clue what to say next.

"I don't steal." she says again.

"In a world where family is all you got," her father starts, "it won't ever do you no good to keep running away. And just to let you know, that money you found on the mantelpiece last time before you ran away was put there for you. I love you darling, but it's gonna be hard for any other man to love you until you learn to love yourself."

Two nights later, Tonya is up at three o'clock in the morning packing the car. She doesn't have any money, nor does she have a clue where she and Taylor are going next, but she knows it's time for her to leave home again.

After the car is packed with all their clothes and some leftovers from the fridge, Tonya makes her way back to her old bedroom to wake up Taylor.

"Wake up baby…" she whispers in his little ear.

Taylor wipes his eyes and looks up at his mother.

"Are you ready to go, love?" she asks him.

"I was born ready mama." he replies with a sleepy smile.

As they make their way to the front door Tonya notices a white envelope on the edge of the mantelpiece.

"Go get in the car baby." she tells Taylor.

As he walks outside, she retrieves the envelope full of money from the mantelpiece. As she smiles down at the envelope she can feel her father's eyes watching her.

"Oh dad," she runs into his protective arms, "I stayed fifty whole hours this time dad."

They both smile as they hug.

"I love you darling," Willy tells her, "but we both know this ain't where your heart is. So, you go find that dream you're chasing, and any time you get lost… you follow that country star back home again baby girl, we'll be here."

Two and a half months later Tonya finds herself in a smelly old motel bathroom in Nashville Tennessee, applying cheap makeup to her almost gorgeous face again.

It's 5:55 PM and she's supposed to be at work at the diner across the street by six. As she makes her way through the front room of the motel she cuts the TV off and then tucks Taylor in the bed.

"Now remember baby," Tonya says, "You can't make any noise while mommy is gone, because you're not supposed to be in here by yourself. So be very quiet so mama won't get in any trouble."

"Okay mama." Taylor replies staring at the raggedy old radio next to the bed.

As Tonya closes the motel door behind her, she listens at the door for a second. Almost instantly she hears him cut the radio on real low.

She smiles, and then slides her room key in her apron pocket as she makes her way across the street to the diner.

As soon as she walks in the diner she sees her manager Cliff staring at her. He points at her and then to his office. As she walks inside he steps in behind her and closes the door.

"You're late." he says.

"You told me to be here at six, Cliff..." she protests.

"Did I," he smiles a slick smile, "Well now I'm saying you were supposed to be here at five."

"I'm sure," Tonya grudgingly removes her apron, "guess this means I have to do "over time" again huh."

"My, you are smart girl." Cliff flips the office light switch off.

Five and a half hours later after the diner is already closed Tonya quickly makes her way across the street to the motel. As soon as she slides the key in the door a strange feeling comes over her.

She opens the door and quickly cuts on the lights.

He's gone.

Tonya screams out. She quickly throws her purse down on the floor spilling her tips everywhere. Then she runs out of the motel room forgetting to lock the door behind her as she rushes towards the front lobby.

As she approaches the hotel lobby that is attached to a restaurant and bar inside she notices there are more people here tonight than usual.

All the people seem to be excited and crowded around something or somebody important. Looking at the huge crowd gives Tonya chilling flashbacks from her days on the country music circuit.

Her heart is racing faster than it ever has before as she nears the crowd.

From behind she can feel somebody grabbing her arm. As she turns around she finds the short Mexican cleaning lady, Rosa.

"Ms. Tonya," Rosa says, "your son Taylor is amazing. Why didn't you tell us he can sing?"

"He can?" Tonya frowns.

"Like an angel…" Rosa explains.

"Look…" Rosa takes her by the hand and leads her through the crowd.

The closer she gets she can hear his powerful little country voice; the pure natural talent is obvious.

There standing in the middle of the bar Tonya sees her son singing beautifully to a crowd full of strangers.

"Damn," Tonya says, "He's almost better than his father."

"Yeah he's really good," Rosa says, "And the man up there next to him is…"

"Bradley Neal," Tonya gasps, "he's the hottest agent in country music today!"

"So I guess you've heard of him..." Rosa laughs.

Tonya makes her way through the rest of the crowd and stands there right in front of her amazing son as he hits every note in his version of, *"Bless the Broken Road"* by country super group Rascal Flatts.

"May God bless the broken roooooooooad...? That led me straight to yoooouuu..." Taylor finishes the song and looks down at his mother with wide eyes.

"I'm sorry mama," he cries, "I didn't wanna leave the room. But Miss Rosa made me come in here and sing for Mr. Neal. She said she hears me singing in the room from outside our door every night."

"That's right," Mr. Neal steps forward to shake Tonya's hand, "And you owe Rosa a huge thank you, Ms. Little. It is Ms. isn't it?"

"It is..." Tonya blushes bright red.

"Fine, fine woman you are," Mr. Neal steps back to look Tonya, "Well darlin', Ms. Rosa brought your son in here, and the boy absolutely blew me away with the very first note he sang. I'm gonna make you a very rich woman Ms. Little... That is if you'll let me."

"Wow," Tonya gasps, "I don't... I really don't know what to..."

"You know exactly what to say," Mr. Neal picks Taylor up off the bar into his arms, "I wanna get Taylor signed and take him all around the country and then the world... they'll call him "Taylor Little" ... The Littlest Country Star..."

"This can't be happening right now," Tonya mumbles, fanning herself fiercely, "Stuff like this doesn't happen to people like us."

"Well Ms. Little, I think it just did." Mr. Neal smiles again.

"What do you think Taylor," she reaches up to kiss his hand, "Are you ready for this baby?"

Taylor looks at Mr. Neal, and then back down into his mother's teary blue eyes.

"I told you mama," he smiles bigger than ever; "I was born ready."

"LITTLEST COUNTRY STAR"

TWINKLE TWINKLE LITTLE BOY
SHINE ON THIS EARTH WITH YOUR JOYFUL NOISE
LIFT EVERY VOICE AND SING
BRINGING FORTH TO US ALL
MAGNIFICENT NEW DREAMS
PRESSURE AND PAIN CREATE NEW PASSION
AS TRUE TALENT CREATES LEGACY EVERLASTING
BORN FROM TWO SEPARATE HEARTS
A PURE SOUL WILL MAKE ITS UNDYING MARK

PIGGY

"Piggy!" the scream comes from downstairs, "Piggy get yo ass up, it's almost time for school!"

The young girl exhales deeply as she adjusts her tight purple shirt and dingy baby blue sweatpants.

As I roll over in my almost too small bed I wish I could sleep the entire day away. Even if I did sleep the whole day away I'd be angry at myself, because I'd be sure I gained another twenty pounds or so lying around all day.

And I know gaining that amount of weight in a day isn't possible, but all the negative stuff I hear on a daily basis is a lot easier for me to believe than the rare encouragement I've heard over the slow lonely years. Have you ever noticed that it's much easier to believe the negative things people say about you than the positive things?

My name is Jordan Hines, but everybody calls me Piggy. I'm eleven years old and I'm a little over weight for my age.

Okay, honestly, I'm really, really fat, but it's not my fault. My mother is fat and all we eat is meat, and sugar... and cakes and pies, and other shit we have no business eating.

I'm just a kid, how can I decide or change my own eating habits? I don't have a job or any cash. I'm only in the fifth grade, so I just don't think it's fair that I get talked about and bullied at school every single day just because I'm fat. I did not, and I am not making myself fat.

"Piggy!" the scream is closer this time, "if you don't get your fat **nasty** ass downstairs right now I'm going to beat you!"

"Okay Mama..."

How can she call me fat? I don't think my miserable mother has even seen her feet in over 15 years. Her entire bedroom smells like Cheetos, pork rinds, and burnt bologna. She is the rudest, unhappiest, Black woman on the planet. I don't understand how she could ever think that I'll end up being better than her with the way the she treats me. But then I guess I know she doesn't really care.

The bathroom floor is cold to my touch. Every time I come in here I try to do everything I can to try not to even look in the mirror. I do everything else I have to do to take care of my business in here, trying my hardest not to assault my own eyes with me.

I think the hardest part about being me... is knowing that even though I am disgustingly huge, it's not even my fault. And maybe, just maybe if I had a father around... maybe he would stand up to my mother and stop her from verbally and physically abusing me. I can't even really be mad at the bullies at school, I mean they're terrible but still not half as bad as my mom, and she gave birth to me. Maybe, a real dad would change all that. But if I did have a father, he would probably hate me too. I mean, why wouldn't he?

32

De'Lure

The water in the sink is warm but not too hot. As I lather my towel with soap I stare into my own eyes knowing full well nobody is ever going to love me or tell me I'm beautiful. I know I'm just a kid, but I am already a slave to my own mind.

The teachers don't understand it. They say I'm way too intelligent for my age. It's simple to me though, I have no friends and no family that give a damn about me. So I spend all my time reading and learning. My future, if I have one at all, will be based on and measured by my economic success and status.

If I don't have money, I will die alone. No man is ever going to want me for just me. I use every day as a training course for the rest of my life. I know full well that the same way the little boys in my class are absolutely repulsed by me, grown men will react to me this way forever... if I live that long.

"Piggy!" her mother yells opening her bedroom door in a too small shirt and saggy dark green leggings, "I'm about to beat yo little fat black ass! I don't give a damn what those bitches at that school say, you ain't smart... You're just as dumb as me. You ain't gonna be shit, just like I ain't shit! I don't know who your daddy is, but whoever that mother fucka' is he ain't shit either!"

"Mama," Piggy says, "you don't know who my father is?"

"Hell no," her mother laughs as her exposed, large, black belly jiggles to the beat of her laughter, "I didn't want none of them men, and they damn sure didn't want me. You know damn well you were a mistake, if I had the money..."

"Mama shut up!" Piggy yells, "don't say that! I know you don't like me, but you do love me!"

"Little girl," her mother says solemnly, "I don't give a damn about you. But what I am going to do... is go back downstairs and finish eating my pork and beans, and when I come back up in five minutes, if you're not ready for school, I'm going to beat your ass like a grown woman. Now I don't give a damn if you pay attention in class or not, but I ain't going to jail again because of you skippin' school. Wait a few more years then you can drop out like your brothers did."

Piggy shakes her head.

"I don't give a damn how you feel, you better stop shaking yo big ass head and hurry the fuck up!" her mother demands. As soon as her mother is gone Piggy rushes to the bathroom wall and snatches the light switch down. Then in the new darkness she rushes back to the sink and opens the top drawer. After she grabs it she falls down to her knees. Her chubby black face is covered in life-threatening tears. As she closes her dark eyes, her mind is racing as violent adrenaline pumps through her veins with a real blood thirst.

Downstairs her mother is laid up in a soiled, old, La-Z-Boy chair watching the Maury Povich show. Piggy's mother doesn't have a care in the world as she repeatedly stuffs a rusty spoon in her mouth covered with cold pork and beans. She's not even chewing; she's swallowing the spoonful's whole.

Her heart stops. She drops the large bowl on the floor and it quickly cracks into several pieces spilling her pork and beans everywhere. She jumps up as fast as her heavy body will allow her to, from the dusty old La-Z-Boy chair. She cuts both of her feet on sharp fragments of the broken bowl, but she's too numb to feel the pain now.

One by one she takes the steps back upstairs towards her daughter's bedroom. As she walks the only reason she knows she's still breathing is because her heart is beating in her ears. She's talking but she can't hear or understand her own words. Her ears and her heart are ringing in tandem from the terrifying noise she heard just moments ago.

As she pushes her daughter's door open, her hands are

shaking fiercely.

Step-by-step she inches closer to her daughter's bathroom door. She grabs hold of the knob. Because of her shaking hand she's not quite able to turn it. With both hands on the knob now she turns it and pushed it open.

The site she sees before her on the bathroom floor turns her blood ice cold. There on her chubby knees in front of her, Piggy is pointing the recently fired gun at her.

"Piggy, what the hell are you doing!" her mother screams, "You shot a hole in my roof?"

"My name is Jordan," the child replies, "You will never call me Piggy again, or talk to me like I'm nothing."

"Go to hell Piggy, you don't scare me bitch!" her mother yells stepping towards her.

"Mama," Piggy cries holding her hand out to warn her, "I love you because you're my mama… but I hate you just as much as you hate me!"

Without another word Piggy fires two shots into her mother's large thick stomach. Her mother falls down instantly

Piggy stands up slowly and approaches her mother's body. As she stands over her, she can see that her mother is bleeding from her mouth and her ears.

When the bullets hit her she fell back hitting her head on the hard tile floor.

As the 11-year-old stands there over her dying mother, she can smell her mother's body relieving itself. The pungent odor is almost too much for the child, but she's so filled with hatred and rage nothing can stop her now.

"Piggy," her pitiful mother cries up to her, "why…"

Piggy fires one more shot into her mother's head ending it all. Then she kneels down close to her and closes her mother's dark eyes.

As Piggy makes her way back towards the toilet stool, every step she takes is heavier than the one before.

Bending down in front of the toilet Piggy begins to vomit uncontrollably. When she's finally done there is residue from her vomit on the toilet seat and on the floor around the stool. Nonetheless Piggy sits on the toilet without cleaning it off first. The wet vomit she feels on her upper thighs feels disgustingly slimy.

Piggy looks over at her mother one last time. The look in her young teary eyes is a mix of love, hatred, power, regret, and satisfaction.

Piggy grabs the gun off the floor and puts it in her mouth. After saying the Lord's Prayer very slowly, Piggy pulls the trigger.

As Piggy opens her eyes she realizes the gun has no bullets left. She immediately stands up on shaky legs, legs almost as shaky as her mother's hands were when she thought she was about to find her daughter dead on her bathroom floor.

As Piggy lies down on top of her mother's still warm body she continues to cry.

"I'm sorry Mama…" she whimpers.

"PIGGY"

BLACK EYES AND BLACK HAIR
A BLACK SOUL FOR WHICH NO ONE CARES
IT'S NOT FAIR
BUT I DON'T DARE SHOW OR
SUBMIT TO MY OWN DESPAIR
SO WHAT I'M TOO BLACK AND WAY TOO FAT
AND THE ROLLS SMELL PUNGENT
AT THE SMALL OF MY BACK
BUT THERE'S NOTHING AT ALL
SMALL ABOUT ME

De'Lure

EVERYONE WHO EVER KNEW ME
CAN'T HELP BUT DOUBT ME
BUT NO TIME FOR POUTING
I'M ELEVEN YEARS OLD AND I ALREADY
UNDERSTAND THIS WORLD IS NOT ABOUT ME
CURSED WITH A FACE
NOT EVEN A MOTHER CAN LOVE
AND I NEVER HAD A FATHER
SO I'D RATHER DROWN IN MY MOTHER'S BLOOD

Carlton Lotus
(*Underneath the Orchards*)

Prologue

The night air is cold enough to chill anyone's bones tonight. The beautiful dark apple orchards surrounding Lotus Mansion are all swaying rhythmically as the cool breeze brushes past them. Master Jasper Lotus, Carlton's great grandfather and a slave owner, had the apple trees planted in their stunning formation over a hundred years ago.

The mystical orchards spell the proud family name out across the gigantic front yard of the estate, the name that has been synonymous with exceptional wealth and class for many years.

Carlton's grandfather Charles, a black man, was born free due to the fact that his biological father was the owner of the plantation he was born on. Master Lotus vowed that, no son of his would live one day as a slave. His skin tone was obviously darker than Master Lotus' other children, who never seemed to like Charles much, but Master wouldn't allow anyone to treat him as anything less than his son. He ate the finest food, wore the best clothing, and was given a private tutor who taught him everything from arithmetic to reading and writing. Charles was born an exceptional child, and if not for his muddied bloodline would probably have been his father's chosen heir to his sizeable fortune.

Charles' mother Katherine, a slave, was Master's mistress for many years before she became pregnant with Charles. Master loved Katherine with everything he was, but this obvious truth eventually drove his wife Margaret insane.

After Katherine gave birth to her mulatto son Charles, Margaret threatened to leave Master if he didn't have Katherine and her half nigger son hung immediately.

Of course Master refused because Katherine was the woman he truly loved. In another day and time, she would have been his wife, but laws just would not allow such a thing back then.

One night, Master awoke to find Margaret pacing back and forth at the foot of his bed with a large knife in her hand.

She was wearing one of her pretty, white, full body night gowns, covered in fresh blood.

She was pacing eerily as if in some kind of trance. She was also speaking, but her words were almost inaudible. Master called her name several times, but Margaret continued to pace and mumble unknown words and phrases. As Master got closer to her he thought maybe she was praying.

Then he soon realized she wasn't praying at all. Margaret was reciting the Bible from the end to the beginning. She was reciting the entire Bible backwards verbatim at a tongue twisting speed.

Crawling slowly out of his bed Master scrambled around quickly to find a shirt and a pair of pants to put on.

Margaret just continued to pace, and preach. In the center of her forehead was an upside down pentagram drawn in blood. Her eyes were rolling in the back of her head as the bloody five-point star dripped down between her demonic eyes.

Approaching her with extreme caution, Master chose his steps carefully. Close enough now to touch her, Master inhales deeply.

Before his breath could leave his mouth as he attempted to exhale, Margaret turned and stabbed him swiftly in the arm.

Master threw her hard to the floor.

"Jasper..." she whispered.

"Margaret what the hell is the matter with you?" he exclaimed checking his fresh wound.

"Do you think He will ever forgive me Jasper?" she asked from her crawling knees.

Master carefully pulls the knife out of his arm.

"Who's gonna forgive you for what Margaret? What have you done woman?" he yelled.

"I killed them..." she recalled.

"You killed who?" Master asked.

"All your niggers... she whispered.

"One by one," she explained, "I took that very knife to them all. It's just us now Jasper. We can manage the grounds ourselves, like God intended. We don't need those filthy black beasts to do what we can do ourselves."

"Woman, have you lost what little brain God gave you?" he fumed.

"Where is Katherine," he asked, "and my son? Where is my boy? What did you do Margaret?"

Master quickly grabbed the candle from his bedside and rushed out of his room to the back door that led out towards the slaves' living quarters. Master ran as fast as his aging legs would carry him. Margaret was close on his heels.

The old dirt path behind the house leading to where the slaves lived seemed longer to Master than it ever had before. From about fifty feet away, he heard a baby crying.

"Charles…" Master Lotus whispered still in full stride.

The first shack he came to was eerily quiet aside from the baby's soft cries in the distance.

Stepping inside the door he saw the slaves' limp bodies all sprawled out on the dirt floor in contorted poses. He rushed to several of the other shacks to find still the same horror.

As he approached the last shack, the baby's cries got louder. Inside he found Katherine's sister, Betty, cradling her newborn daughter.

"Where is my boy?" Master asked.

"I can't say Master." Betty replied solemnly noticing the murderous Margaret standing behind him.

"Betty, what do you mean you can't say?" He asked.

"My lips is sealed Master," she vowed, "Miss Margaret done killed just about everybody I love. I can't lose my only sister's only child too."

Master Lotus stepped closer to Betty so she could see the fire in his eyes.

"Betty where is Katherine and where is my boy?" he asked again.

"Master I can't say…" she repeated.

"Damn it Betty," he screamed, "I'm awake now. And you can rest assured that Miss Margaret ain't gone hit nobody else with this here knife. Now tell me where they are Betty, please girl!"

Betty hesitated leaning forward to look into Margaret's eyes. The sadistic smile on her pale white bloodstained face turned Betty's blood ice cold and sent painful chills down her scrawny spine. Master can see the real fear in Betty's face.

"Margaret, get out of here now!" he demanded without even looking at his evil wife.

"I'm not going anywhere Jasper," Margaret snapped, "I'm not one of your little..."

"Get your ass back to the house now before I take this knife to you!" Master exclaimed.

"You're really something Jasper," she said, "some slave driver you are. You fell in love with your nigger whore and left me to feel..."

"Margaret I don't give a damn what you feel," he bellowed, "Get your ass to that house now!"

She left without another word.

Down on his knees Master looked at Betty with those piercing blue eyes.

He leaned in closely to hear what she had to tell him. After she was finished speaking, he thanked her and left as quickly as he came.

Back on the trail Master was wide open headed back to the big house at top speed.

Once inside he rushed up the stairs all the way to the third floor. He proceeded towards the closed door with caution not knowing what to expect.

Slowly he turned the knob and pushed the door open. Inside he found all of his children Margaret gave birth to sleeping calmly.

In the far corner was Tabitha the maid rocking back and forth gently in the old rocking chair.

At first he thought her eyes were closed but as he made his way closer to her he could see with the help of the moonlight her eyes were fixed directly on him.

Nestled in her protective pale white arms was a small yellow baby.

"Tabs..." he said.

"Yes Jaaasper…" she said.

Tabitha always said his name that way because like every other woman whom ever met old Master, she was absolutely smitten by him.

Master was quite a handsome old bastard in his day.

"Is that my…" he started.

"Yes, Jaaasper this is your son Charles." she smiled down at the boy as if he were her own child.

Master sighed heavily in relief.

Leaning down close to her, Master kissed Tabitha softly on the lips, holding her delicate face in his hands.

"Thanks Tabs, now where is Katherine," he asked, "Is she here? Betty said you would know where she is."

Continuing to rock Tabitha didn't respond.

"Tabs," he said, "Tabs what happened? What did Margaret do to Katherine?"

"She's gone Master." Tabitha told him.

"Dead…" he gasped weakly.

"Better off dead," she replied, "but nawl she gone to Mississippi."

"Mississippi?" he frowned.

"Yessir," Tabs confirmed, "the Mistress sold her to the Baker brothers late last night for real cheap. God knows what they gone do to that pretty girl on the way to Mississippi. Them Baker boys are a real nasty piece of work Jaaasper."

"I know," he said then looked at her with those eyes, "Why didn't you come get me Tabs?"

"Master I just couldn't," she told him, "Miss Katherine made me swear I wouldn't leave this room, or let a soul touch little Charles until you came looking for us."

"Well if you were in here, how do you know what happened to Katherine? How do you know she's not dead?" he asked.

"Oh I know everything that happened Jaaasper," she said, "I could hear the crazy screams from those poor black bastards' way down yonder. They didn't even fight her Jaaasper. They all let her kill them without even trying to fight back."

"And what about Katherine," he said, "How do you know about Katherine?"

"Well I was standing right there by the big window," she said, "and I heard Mrs. Lotus down below talking to Donald Baker. She told him she wanted Miss Katherine taken deep down in the woods of Mississippi where you would never be able to find her. She said what they were going to do to her down there would be much worse than death."

"What was the last thing Katherine said to you?" he asked. "Nothing that I can recall," Tabitha says, "wait... she said to tell you that the sun always rises on the hill near the bayou, or something like that."

"On the bayou..." he smiled, "you sure she said on the bayou?"

"Yessir." Tabitha replied.

"My boy..." he said looking down at the baby.

"Yes Jasper and he's beautiful." Tabitha replies.

"He is I suppose, but the third son is the one I'm waiting for," Jasper explained, "This boy has to be preserved so his son can be born. His grandson is the one who will retrieve the Lotus diamond and return it to me."

Master kissed Tabitha softly on the lips again, and then kissed little Charles on the head before leaving them to finish his business with his wife.

All the house workers watched in silent happiness as Master dragged Margaret away from the big house kicking and screaming like a child.

That next morning Master Lotus had all of the slaves' bloody bodies buried right there underneath the orchards.

Above their bloody graves he had gorgeous purple lotus flowers planted. No one ever saw or spoke of Margaret again.

I read all of that in my Great-grandfather's journal that he kept up until the day he left Lotus Mansion. He passed it down to my grandfather, then he down to my father, and finally my father passed it down to me. My Great-grandfather Jasper went missing on his forty-third birthday, never to be seen or heard from again. Some people say Margaret's ghost came back to get him. Some say he spent the rest of his days searching for Katherine. Others say he and Katherine had been communicating for years just waiting for the perfect time to meet up, and run away together. None of us will ever really know the truth though. Just days before GG Jasper disappeared; he gave everything he owned to my grandfather Charles Lotus. He told everybody currently living at the Lotus estate that in his absence they were to refer to young Charles as Master, and do exactly as he said no questions asked.

Chapter 1

My grandfather Charles wasn't a bad person, but he was very different from his father. Because of the jealousy he endured from his white brothers and sisters during his upbringing he developed a defined chip on his slender shoulders.

He wasted no time purchasing properties outside of his estate for his half brothers and sisters whom he no longer wanted to live on his property.

People in town considered him an uppity nigger. This fact

never bothered Charles, largely because he was too wealthy to care. People everywhere could say any malicious thing they wanted to about him, but none could deny how rich, handsome, and dangerously charming he was. The only thing Charles got from Jasper other than his fortune was his unmistakable steel blue eyes.

Charles was only seventeen years old when Jasper left him with everything, so it was only natural that he ran things like a young man would. Charles was no push over; he ran the Lotus Estate with an 'iron fist'.

He also ushered in a new era of Lotus style and life. Since no one on the plantation knew if or when Master was ever coming back, they didn't dare question young Charles' authority.

Charles took over command of the estate in 1863, slavery was over, but most people's mindsets in the South had not changed at all.

His main lover and best friend was the maid Tabitha. Tabitha, now thirty-two years old never got over Jasper's sudden disappearance. At first nothing seemed to ease the pain of his absence, but when she looked in Charles' eyes she found all the comfort she needed; in the soothing crystal eyes that Jasper blessed his youngest son with.

Every time Charles made love to his father's maid, he felt empowered. Every time he took her he felt like he was making the old man proud. In his mind he was in total control, picking up right where his father left off.

Charles wanted to make his father proud, but he also wanted to live his life to its fullest extent.

Master wasn't much for large gatherings at the big house. Charles on the other hand, threw several large parties every week. Only those of exceptional class and wealth, who received special invitations from him, displaying the Lotus family insignia were allowed to attend.

On the night of each party Charles would have the young cook Mason, to prepare grandiose meals with assorted dishes.

Mason was as blind as a bat, but he was an exceptional cook nonetheless.

Jasper put him in his kitchen at a very young age surrounded by old black women who taught him all the basics of cooking. At the age of fourteen Mason began running the kitchen as the head cook.

After the food was ready Charles would ride into the city and pick up five of the prettiest local girls he could find. He would buy them expensive gowns then bring them home to be used as eye candy and party favors for his rich guests.

The prettiest local girl at the party would be invited by Charles to stay at his house for seven days. The lucky lady of his choosing would be spoiled and showered with extravagant gifts for those seven days. On the eighth day no matter how pretty the girl was she would always be dropped back off in the dirty, poor streets of the inner city; forced back into the reality of her true circumstances, and made to leave all of her lavish gifts behind at the big house.

At twenty-six years of age, Charles' favorite party girl gave birth to his only child he ever had. A son, he named him Caden.

"LOTUS"

BACK IN A TIME WHEN COLOR MATTERED MORE
THAN CHARACTER
THE RICH JUST GOT RICHER PALE FACES ALL THE
MERRIER
PURE SOULS WERE BLOTTED OUT BY BLIND HATRED
THE DARK FACES JUST HAD TO FACE IT
THERE WAS NO PLACE OR ROOM HERE FOR THEM
TO PHASE IN
BOUGHT AND SOLD BY OUR SLAVE MASTERS
OUR STORIES TOLD THROUGH BLOOD STAINED
CHAPTERS
SLAUGHTERED BY THE JEALOUS WIFE IN OUR SLEEP
THE STRONG BLADE DRIPPING RED AS SHE PLUNGE
IT SO DEEP
BUT THE CHILD STILL LIVES ON AND THE FORTUNE
WILL FIND HIM
ALL THE PURE WHITE SOULS WILL ONE DAY BE
FORCED TO MIND HIM
BORN OF MIXED BLOOD STILL A PRINCE IN HIS OWN
RIGHT
HE NEVER KNEW THE TERROR OR THE SCREAMS
LOST THAT NIGHT
AS WE STARE UP FROM UNMARKED GRAVES
AND THE LOTUS FLOWERS AND APPLES BLOOM
ABOVE US
OUR TEARS PRAYERS AND DREAMS
WILL NEVER AMOUNT TO MORE THAN BLACK DUST

BLACK CUPID

"Love is as love does, love drains you… and forces you to suck and drown on your own blood. Love is a drug and a skill, it's a painful battlefield stained with the art of kill or be killed. Never show me your heart or mistake me for stupid, you'll lose your love and your life at the hands of Black Cupid!!!"

"1, 2, 3, 4, 5, 6, 7, 8, 9, 10…" the doctor counts slowly in his head over, and over, and over again.

"This is not working!" he screams.

"Kathleen," the doctor cries out, "Kathleen baby… Baby, please answer me. I know, baby I know we're not perfect… Hell we're not even good right now, but everything can and will get much better..."

As he looks around his dark empty room he slowly realizes again that she's gone. She left him alone to die. He screams out at the top of his voice. Pain and misery are the only constants in his life, they are the only two things he wakes up knowing he can count on being right there waiting for him.

(Dr. Brown)

My name is Dr. Herald Brown. I was born here in Orlando, Florida. I went to the University of Harvard in Cambridge, Massachusetts to study psychology. After graduation I moved home to Orlando to start a marriage counseling practice.

In 2009, I married a beautiful young woman from Tampa, Florida named Kathleen Truelove; of all the things that woman could have been named.

We had a wonderful marriage for seven years. Because of the popularity of my books and my private counseling practice, she and I were given the opportunity to host a television show together based on my private practice.

Everything seemed so magical, until the second Kathleen broke my heart. She used me, she cheated on me multiple times, and then she left me. I was humiliated. My business suffered. Who wants to pay for a publically divorced marriage counselor? Nobody that's who! Kathleen was a part of my brand; she was a part of me!

She even took my kids, now all I have left is my sick dark depression. That evil bitch ruined me, and she said it's because I no longer satisfied her.

He's had enough of the loud silence yet again; he quickly slams his fist down on his bed in a sudden fit of rage. Out of his bed moving swiftly across his cold floor, he pulls on some black leather sweatpants and a black body shirt. The shirt is sleeveless showing his expensive new arm tattoos. Both of his toned arms are littered with tattoos, mostly hearts, angels, and arrows of various sizes. The majority of the hearts are broken or bleeding.

Sitting at the edge of his bed he carefully slides on a pair of black socks, and then he straps on his heavy black combat boots.

"Love is as love does," the doctor mumbles coldly to himself, "love drains you... and forces you to suck and drown on your own blood!!!"

From beneath his bed he grabs his weapon of choice and then tightly straps it to his back. He can smell blood already. Someone... some inconsiderate woman has to lose her life tonight because her death is the only medicine that can ease his pain right now.

As he exits his home the only thing he can hear are his own words swirling around inside his head amongst the pounding of his bleeding heart. Never take love away from a man who lives and breathes it.

As he walks he smiles to himself. He's not happy, but he is pleased that he lives inside the city and never has to work hard to find a victim. After walking several blocks from his home he spies a young black couple sitting inside a fancy restaurant.

He takes a comfortable seat on a bench across the street from the restaurant. As he studies the couple, the evil grin on his face is slowly becoming painful. He reaches up to massage his hairy face. As he touches his face he realizes he hasn't shaved or even bathed for several days now.

It doesn't matter, nothing matters... In fact, the only thing that does matter is ridding the world of lying, cheating, backstabbing bitches!

As three white college girls walk by, they smile at him. He doesn't understand why they're smiling. The doctor has long forgotten how naturally attractive he is and has always been to the opposite sex. He growls at them like an untamed animal.

"What the hell!" one of the girls screams as the three of them scamper across the street.

As he refocuses his attention on the couple in the restaurant across the street, he's waiting for the young lady to show any sign of unfaithfulness.

From his pocket the doctor takes out a pair of binoculars. The man and woman are both very attractive. They each have on wedding bands, so they're obviously married to each other. Doc sheds one reminiscent tear.

As he looks on, the young black couple is staring into each other's eyes now and they appear to be lost in true unwavering love. More importantly they seem to be in equal love. Doc used to teach people about being in "equal love" long ago. His idea of true love was that both people should love each other on the exact same level. This accomplishment would alleviate any chance of heartbreak… at least in the doctor's old mind.

The man in the restaurant excuses himself from the table. After he's gone the young woman makes sure he's gone and then she reaches down inside her purse. The doctor figures she's pulling out a mirror to check her makeup, but on the contrary she pulls out her cell phone and hands it to their server. The tall white man obligingly enters his phone number into the little jezebel's phone.

The doctor can feel his temperature rising dramatically. His heart rate is at an all-time high now. This woman has just signed her death certificate and doesn't even have a clue that she's done so.

From behind his back, the doctor pulls a sharp, black, steel reinforced arrow, with a heart-shaped head. He positions it in his powerful crossbow, and then leans forward aiming it at the woman's head. She's probably about a hundred feet away from him.

As her date returns to the table she smiles up at him as if nothing happened in his absence. The man bends down to kiss her deceitful lips one final time.

Aim, fire, hit!

The arrow soars through the air at an unreal speed and crashes straight through the front window of the restaurant and into the beautiful skull of the young unfaithful woman.

She died instantly but the doctor didn't wait around to make sure. He's long gone still enjoying the high from his last hit of pure, blood thirst quenching, ecstasy.

BLACK CUPID

THE DARKNESS IS GROWING STRONGER
AS THE ARROW SPLITS THE AIR
THERE'S NO MORE BEAUTIFUL SOUND
THAN IT PIERCING HER SKULL AS NEW BLOOD
STAINS HER HAIR
THEY NEVER KNOW WHAT HITS THEM
THE DEATH THEY MEET IS QUICK
IF YOU DON'T KNOW THE LANGUAGE OF LOVE
YOU'LL FIND MY THOUGHTS QUITE SICK
BUT MY HEART BEATS HARDER THAN YOURS
MY BLOOD AND SOUL ARE PURE
BUT IF YOU CHOOSE NOT TO BE A FAITHFUL WIFE
BLACK CUPID KNOWS THE ONLY CURE
AS THEIR BLOOD AND SOULS LEAVE THEIR EVIL
BODIES THE REAPER LIES IN WAIT
TO SNATCH THEM DOWN TO THE DEPTHS OF HELL
AND BLACK CUPID OPENS THE GATE

Truly Tainted

"Alice... Alice where are you?" Barbara whispers into the darkness.

No response.

Barbara straightens her long floral print dress, and carefully pulls her long black hair into a ponytail.

"Alice..." she whispers again.

Alice doesn't respond but Barbara can hear her giggling somewhere in the distance.

As she continues to walk deeper into her best friend's home Barbara is careful not to make any noise.

Suddenly, Barbara hears a door swinging open nearby.

"Jason, you are a mess..." Alice says in the deceitful darkness.

"Ms. Alice," Jason says, "you have no idea how long I've been waiting to feel that..."

Barbara flips a light switch on. There standing in front   of her she sees her best friend of thirty years, in a short skirt standing next to a young man who is clearly not her husband.

"Barbs..." Alice squints to get a clearer view of her intruder.

"Jason Wallace," Barbara says with a hand on each hip, "boy where the hell is your mother and father? It doesn't matter, get the hell out of this house right now damn it!"

"Yes ma'am..." he rushes towards the front door after zipping his dark denim pants up.

"Now Barbs, why did you scare the poor kid like that?" Alice calmly wipes the old smeared red lipstick from around her mouth.

Barbara steps closer to Alice. "Alice, what the hell were you doing in the closet with that boy?"

"What's done in the dark...?" Alice's giggling fit returns.

"This is not funny, Alice," Barbara assures her, "now where
is Brice?"

"Brice..." Alice says.

"Yeah Brice," Barbara says, "Your husband Brice..."

"Oh Brice," Alice frowns looking down to cover her partially exposed left breast, "Brice is um, I don't know Barbs, but calm down girl everything's going to be just fine."

"Alice, you're drunk, and why the hell were you in the closet with that boy? Answer me, now!" Barbara demands.

"Would you stop saying that, Barbs," Alice replies, "He's twenty-three years old, he's not a boy anymore."

"He's the preacher's son Alice," Barbs yells, "And you're thirty-five! This is not okay!"

"Well, I'm sorry." Alice says.

"You're sorry," Barbara replies, "What the hell is that supposed to do? It's damn sure not gonna undo what you just did!" "Damn it, Barbs..." Alice stumbles forward trying not to let her wrinkled stretched halter top slip down again.

After collapsing in a nearby chair Alice tries to remember what she was going to say.

"Barbs," Alice slurs, "You don't know... and you don't understand anything! You always think you're so perfect and you're always right. Hell girl, you think you're holier than Jesus Christ himself!"

"Are you serious right now Alice?" Barbara interjects.

"Yes," she replies, "I'm not you, Barbs! My life isn't perfect and neither am I. Sometimes, I get drunk and do random things in closets with random men."

Alice burst into disturbing laughter.

"Alice," Barbara reaches down to grab her best friend's sweaty hand, "This is not at all funny and I'm not perfect love. I'm just concerned about you..."

"Don't be," Alice snaps, "you can't possibly understand what I'm going through, so don't worry your pretty little head about me."

"Oh really," Barbs replies, "I've been faithfully married to the same man for fifteen years, so anything and everything you and Brice are going through now I've felt or already gone through, Alice..."

"Leave me alone Barbs!" Alice yells, snatching her hand away from her.

"Now, Alice you know I can't do that love..." Barbara replies calmly.

"You can and you will," Alice tells her, "I am not wrong, and you will not force me to feel bad about what I've done!"

"Alice you're cheating on your husband..." Barbara tells her friend.

"So what, Barbs," Alice says, "We all know what this is... Well, everybody except for your blind ass that is."

"And what the hell is that supposed to mean?" Barbara asks.

"Nothing..." Alice turns away from her confused friend.

"Damn it, Alice you tell me what the hell you're trying to say right damn now!"

She doesn't respond.

Barbara steps around in front of Alice.

Wham!

Barbara slaps Alice hard across her mouth.

"Tell me, now!" she demands.

"Fine," Alice screams still in shock from the slap, "I'm cheating on him... he's cheating on me... Jefferson is cheating on you, and you're the only bump on a log sitting with her legs closed so tight your freakin' ovaries can't even breathe... which is probably why you never could get pregnant..."

Barbara's mouth drops, she quickly turns around to shield her face from Alice.

"Barbs, I'm sorry," Alice says, "I... I didn't, you know I didn't mean that."

"Jefferson is not cheating on me..." Barbara cries.

"He is honey," Alice says, "You and me... we're just trophies to them. We're just the mainstays in our husband's lives. They work and make all the money and what do we do? That's a real question Barbs... You answer the question for me, love. What do we do?"

"We stay home..." Barbara starts.

"We sit at home," Alice interjects, "we just sit at home and attempt to be perfect, white suburban housewives. But our husbands are so rich we can't even do that. They pay someone to do everything! Barbs, I don't even know where to find a fork in my own damn kitchen. That's sick Barbs. And we can't even begin to complain because we don't have any money or real education... and we don't have a clue about how to support ourselves. So we just stay..."

"Jefferson is not cheating on me..." Barbara repeats.

Alice shakes her head at her best friend.

"Let it go, Barbs," Alice tells her, "I know for a fact Jefferson is cheating on you…"

"And how could you possibly know that?" Barbara wipes away new tears.

"Because Barbs." she replies.

"Because what bitch," Barbara exclaims, "Tell me before I slap you again!"

"Because he's screwing *me*, Barbs…" Alice admits.

Barbara immediately falls down to her aging knees. She can't breathe now or even see for that matter.

Alice starts giggling again.

"What's funny now, you evil lying bitch?" Barbara asks.

"I never lied," Alice laughs snidely, "I never said I wasn't sleeping with your husband, and you never asked. So I'm not the liar, Barbs… Jefferson is."

"You're supposed to be my best friend," Alice says, "this is so sick!"

"Oh, you have no idea," Alice continues to laugh, "And it gets better *love*…"

"What does that mean Alice… it gets better," Barbara cries, "What are you not telling me?

"Might wanna hold your heart and your panties for this one," Alice laughs, "You ain't gon wanna…"

"Alice, you bitch," Barbara screams, "Are you pregnant by my Jefferson? You spit it out now you little evil drunk whore you!"

"I'm not pregnant, I have AIDS." Alice admits.

"No…" Barbara cries, from her swelling bruised knee caps.

"Yep," Alice confirms, "I'm dyin' from full blown *AIDS*! I got it from *your* husband, and then I purposely gave it to my husband's unfaithful lyin' ass!"

Barbara gasps for air.

"We all have **AIDS** Barbs," Alice tells her friend, "But don't worry *you're* safe, Jefferson told me he hasn't even touched you in over four years. I guess that's why he started sneaking over here to see me." Alice laughs again. "Life isn't as perfect as you thought huh, Barbs?"

Barbara can't breathe. Her heart is pounding loudly in her chest. The room is spinning violently as she falls back hard on the tile floor and everything around her slowly turns black.

"TRULY TAINTED"

*MARY HAD A LITTLE LAMB WHOSE FLEECE WAS
WHITE AS SNOW
AND UNDERNEATH THAT SNOW WHITE FLEECE MARY
DIDN'T KNOW
THE LIFE IN WHICH SHE THOUGHT SHE LIVED
WAS MOSTLY JUST FOR SHOW
THE SILENT CRIES AND SCREAMING PAIN
BEGAN TO TAKE CONTROL
DECEPTION LIES AND FAIRYTALES
ARE ALL THAT MARY KNOWS
STAR CROSSED LOVE MUST ALWAYS END
THAT'S JUST HOW THE STORY GOES
THE BITTER TRUTH PAINTS AN AWKWARD MOMENT
THAT MARY MIGHT NOT SURVIVE
BUT SHE COULD NEVER GO BACK
INTO HER HUSBANDS ARMS
EVEN IF SHE TRIED
HE'S FAR TOO GONE NOW
BUT HE HAD HIS CHANCE TO CHOOSE
NOW DEATH WINS OUT WITHOUT A FIGHT
THE DISEASE WILL NEVER LOSE*

Disobedient

This kitchen is a mess. Ain't nobody in this house working but me, but I gotta clean, cook, and then clean up after I cook. Shaking my damn head, I can't believe how they treat me. Oh well, at least I got a man.

Janet fakes a smile as she enters her den and makes her way towards her piece of a man.

"Janet," Rico, her muscle bound boyfriend stresses, "you know damn well that girl is too old to not be working already!"

"Are we still talking about this bae…?" Janet sighs. "Hell yes," he replies, "Did that lil bitch get a job yet?"

Janet chooses her words wisely as she looks at his massive 6'4 body frame.

"She's only seventeen Rico," Janet replies, in an almost childish tone, "You're acting like she's thirty something. Give my baby a break please."

"I'm not acting like anything," Rico stands up from the sofa to look down at Janet, "I know exactly how old she is. She's seventeen, that's two years older than you were when you had her!"

"So…" Janet stands up to face him.

"Don't talk back to me, Janet," Rico yells, "My point is, if you were able to grow up at fifteen and be responsible, she damn sure should be able to at seventeen!"

Janet quickly sits back down as the glare on Rico' face instantly shatters the momentary confidence she mustered up

"She will get a job baby…" Janet looks up at her overbearing man with uncertain eyes.

"No, she won't," Rico points towards the back room, "That little bitch has no respect for me or you. And this apartment may be in your name, but I pay the majority of the bills. She's going to start treating me with respect, you both are!"

"Okay." Janet mumbles softly.

"Okay what…" he kneels down close to her with a hideous scowl on his hard brown face.

"Okay, Daddy Rico…" she says.

"Mom," Jade yells from the back room, "*Moooooom!*"

Jade walks in the front room of the tiny apartment to find her mother's hulking boyfriend lying on top of her.

"Ugh," Jade says, "Um, don't y'all have a *fucking* room?" "Watch your mouth little girl!" Rico demands.

"No." she snaps back at him.

"Jade what's wrong now," her mother asks, "Why are you screaming my name? I know there's nothing really wrong."

"It's Friday mom," Jade says, "the

movies…" "There's money in my purse,
Jade." Janet
sighs.

"Um," Jade says, "Do I look like I read minds? I do not know where you keep that raggedy ass bag at."

"Wait a minute," Rico says, "I bought your mother that purse from my homeboy, **New York,** on the corner…"

"Exactly," Jade rolls her eyes at him, "Mom, where is your bag, so I can get my money."

"You don't have any money little girl," Rico says, "That's your mother's money. You don't have a job… so yo ass don't have any money."

"And who was talking to you?" Jade rolls her neck and curls her upper lip.

"Mom…" Jade whines.

"Look on the floor by my bed Jade." Janet tells her daughter.

As he watches her storm away in her tiny shorts and tank top Rico imagines several ways he can teach her a lesson.

"You're babying her Janet." Rico huffs, agitatedly.

"She'll be fine," Janet claims, "Now let me get up, it's almost time for me to go to work."

"Whatever." Rico lies back on the sofa and cuts the television on.

Rico's phone vibrates. He smiles as he reads the text.

In the back room of the apartment, Janet is finishing getting dressed for work. She definitely hates both of her jobs, and could afford to quit one of them if her daughter wasn't such a slave to fashion.

Jade always wants something else, but is rarely satisfied. As Janet contemplates her slow, sad, quiet life she's hoping and praying that her daughter will have a much better adult existence than hers.

After tying up both of her slip resistant shoes, Janet flips her light switch down and leaves her room. She slowly passes by her daughter's room, and then doubles back. After knocking several times and receiving no response, Janet turns the knob and opens Jade's door.

As she looks inside she finds her teenage daughter posing provocatively as she snaps pictures of herself with her new smart phone.

"Jade," Janet exclaims, "What the hell are you doing?" "Damn," Jade stumbles to the floor in embarrassed, frustration, "Do you ever knock mom, damn!"

"I knocked three times," Janet says, "And I know damn well you weren't planning to post those pictures on Instagram…" "No mom," Jade stands up from the floor in her underwear, "Did you want something, lady?" Janet stares at her beautiful daughter trying hard to find the words to say to make her understand that she is not her enemy but her biggest supporter.

"Jade baby," Janet says, "What is wrong with you? Is this my fault? Just tell me what I did and I'll…"

"No mom," Jade groans, "God, mom please don't start crying again, damn."

"I know we don't have a perfect life here…" Janet starts. "Duh," Jade interjects, "Anything else lady? I was busy when you busted in my room like the police."

"No Jade," Janet says, "There's nothing else. Just know that Mama loves you, and if you ever need to talk…"

"Blah, blah, blah," Jade interjects again, "Yeah mom, if I ever need to talk I won't bother, because you had me at what fifteen, and grandma allowed that dumb shit to happen, so I won't be calling her old ass either. Don't worry about me. I'll just thug it out for now. Now please get out, this is very awkward right now."

As Janet looks down at the cluttered floor of her daughter's room she knows damn well she's the one who created this spiteful, disrespectful monster.

She turns and closes her door without another word. As she stands there outside of her daughter's bedroom she still has the doorknob clutched tightly in her palm. As a couple of warm tears begin to stream down her face, she can hear Rico in the other room getting up off the sofa.

From the end of the hallway he can see her crying. Rico shakes his head as he walks towards her.

"Come here baby," Rico pulls his woman into his protective arms, "Just go to work love, if you want me to I'll talk to Jade's rude ass for you."

"No, Rico," Janet says, "You don't have to do that. I'm fine, everything is gonna be fine."

Rico walks Janet to the door.

After stepping outside of the door Janet turns around to stare up into Rico's dark eyes.

"Rico," she says, "Do you love me?"

"Baby," he replies, "Just go to work. You know how I feel, I'm never gonna leave you."

Rico bends down and kisses her on her forehead.

"Have a good day, baby," he says, "I'll be here waiting when you get back."

Rico closes the door and then returns to his position on the couch.

On cue Jade walks out of her room and through the front still dressed like she was when her mother caught her taking the racy pictures on her phone. With a faint smile on her face she slowly walks past Rico into the kitchen. He watches every step she takes carefully.

With a water bottle in hand Jade walks back to the front room.

"Damn," Jade looks down at Rico' hulking frame, "I thought that worrisome bitch would never leave."

"Well, she's gone now baby girl," he growls as he pulls her down on top of him, "I love the pictures you just sent me. Now... do that thing Daddy likes."

Jade smiles. She kisses him long and hard.

The front door unlocks from the outside and flies open with no resistance.

"Mom! What the hell..." Jade jumps off the couch and stumbles back quickly.

"Jade, shut the hell up, and go in your room!" Janet demands. For once, the teen does exactly as she's told.

Rico stands up and pretends to dust himself off.

Janet continues to stare down the hall towards her daughter's room. She can feel him staring at her.

"Now you're being a real mom, Janet," he grins, "That's my baby. Good girl, I knew..."

"*Shut the hell up Rico*!" she demands with finality.

"Girl, I know damn well you ain't talking to me..." Rico says crossing his large arms on his chest.

"You lying, cheating, son of a bitch," Janet interjects, "You

lying, cheating, son of a *bitch*!!!"

"Nah, nah baby it's not what it looked like at all," he lies, "that little bitch jumped on me. Every time you leave the house it seems like I have to beat her ass off me with a stick." "Is that what it seems like Rico Sauvé..." she walks towards him noticing the new sweat on his brows. "Hell yeah bae..." Rico lies again.

"If my daughter," Janet starts, "my little innocent teenage daughter *ever* came on to you... why the hell have you never told me Rico?"

Janet slaps him hard across his hard brown face. "I don't know baby..." he frowns.

"Oh, you know," she scoffs after slapping him hard again, "I think we both know why you didn't tell me. You enjoyed it, you sick bastard. You had the cake and wanted to eat the little Debbie too."

"I never touched that girl, Janet... " he lies again.

"Get the hell out of my house Rico," Janet screams pushing him over the edge of her dingy old sofa, "get the hell out and if I ever see you again I will go down as press charges on you immediately!!!"

"You don't gotta do all that," he pleads picking himself up off the floor, "I'm leaving. I just need to go get my money out the room..."

"The money stays, you go," Janet stalks to the door, "Get out!"

Rico flinches as Janet swings hard at him again.

"Mama," Jade opens her door down the hall, "Don't make him leave it's my fault."

"The door is open asshole, get out!" Janet ignores her confused child.

"Mama," Jade cries out, "Mama please... I love him!"

Rico smiles inadvertently at the child down the hallway. "No," Janet screams out, "Get your trifling ass out now!"

After pushing him out into the hallway Janet turns around to find Jade sprawled out on the hall floor crying like her dog just died.

Janet's body feels more than weak; she has nothing left inside her. As she walks around to the front of her smelly

De'Lure

old couch, she realizes things will never be the same between her and Jade again.

"DISOBEDIENT"

A SINK FULL OF DIRTY
DISHES THE FRIDGE
AGAIN IS BARE
FOOD STAMPS DON'T COME FOR 12 MORE
DAYS BUT NO ONE REALLY CARES
THEY EXPECT ME TO PERFORM
MIRACLES IN A KITCHEN FULL OF
NOTHING
I OPENED MY HOUSE WITH EYES WIDE
SHUT I KNEW THAT I WAS RUSHING
MY MAN MOVED IN WITH MY DAUGHTER AND
ME
THE MISTAKE MADE WAS MINE
I CANNOT LIVE AND LOVE MY MAN IN PEACE
MY CHILD WILL NOT COMPLY
AT EVERY TURN SHE GIVES HIM LIP
WHEN HE'S ONLY TRYING TO HELP
MY BIGGEST FEAR IS LOSING HIM
WITHOUT HIM I'VE NOTHING LEFT
32 WITH TWO YOUNG KIDS
NOT EXACTLY THE WIFEY TYPE
BUT I WON'T COMPLAIN OR BEAT ME DOWN
MY CHOICES CREATED MY LIFE

DOMESTICATED

"I am so ugly. No matter what the reflection in this broken mirror tells me I know I am more than undesirable. I have a man, but I don't deserve him. Nope, Tyrone deserves so much better than me. I know he is only keeping me around as a favor to me. He knows nobody else wants me, he tells me every single day. I used to have my doubts, but now I know no man could ever really love me for me. Tyrone has taught me so much over the years. Men only want women like me for one thing. I have to be smart enough to stay and be loyal because he's the only man who will put up with my stupid black ass..."

The door opens quickly.

"Bitch, what the fuck you doing in the mirror?" Tyrone growls in a low guttural tone.

Tyrone stands six foot six and his beer belly is almost as big as his ego. He's dark skinned but not as dark as Denise is.

"Baby," she smiles back at him, "I was combing my hair

you told me to…"

"I told you to fix ya damn face," he snatches his old smelly work boots off, "but only God can fix that ugly mother fucka' and he ain't gone do that no time soon."

Tyrone laughs at his crude joke.

Denise looks back at the broken mirror. Her almost pretty dark face is starting to show wrinkles, mostly from stress. The bruises on her face and on the sides of her head don't help her case much either. She turns back around and looks up at him.

"Wipe that dumbass look off your black ass face," he tears his shirt off and throws it into a pile of unwashed laundry near the bedroom door, "And what the hell do you have on?"

"I," she looks down at her clothing, "these are just my sweats baby… I've just been here at the house all day. I really didn't think…"

"Shut the hell up, Denise," he interjects, "I know you didn't think. You can't think cause I ain't took the time to teach your stupid ass how to think. Look at you…"

Denise wipes a lone tear away from her left eye.

"Look at you," he steps closer to her, "you think after a long day's work this is what a man wants to come home to? And you wonder why I cheat on you as much as I do. You don't turn me on at all Denise, I mean damn it I'm just being honest. You look disgusting to me. Come here!"

She doesn't move.

"Stand up woman!" Tyrone snatches Denise to her unsure feet.

"Tyrone…" she cries.

"Shut up bitch," he growls with his lips pressed to her left ear, "You speak when damn spoken to. You are my mother fuckin' property and I don't give a damn what you think or feel."

"Okay daddy…" she whimpers.

"You oughta be happy." he pulls her large shirt over her

head and then rips her large sweatpants down just far enough.

"I am happy Tyrone." she looks up into his dark eyes with real fear.

"Call me daddy, you dumbass bitch," he yells with her neck gripped tightly in both of his large hands, "and hell yeah you should be happy. Nobody else wants you, I'm doing you..."

"A favor." she interjects with a broken look on her face.

Whap!!!

Tyrone slaps her down to the dirty bedroom floor. As she lays there she doesn't know which one is worse, the stinging pain on the right side of her throbbing face or the stench of the filthy carpet assaulting her almost broken nose.

"Get up!" Tyrone demands.

Denise makes it to her knees and then pauses to pull her sweatpants back up.

"No, you can leave them down," he pulls her up to her feet again, "you ain't gonna need them. Once I'm done with you, you gone go sit on the toilet and push every bit of my seed back out, and then you're gonna get your musty ass in the tub."

"That tub is filthy, Tyrone..." she reminds him.

"Well bitch I know it's filthy, you never clean it!" he pushes her face hard. Denise stumbles back into the mirror.

"Tyrone, there's nothing here to clean with..." she cries out.

"Shut the hell up and get over here," he walks towards the bed, "You always got some dumbass excuse."

"That is not an excuse Tyrone," Denise holds her ground, "I have no money. You work every single day but you don't give me a god damned thing! How the hell can I buy supplies to clean this nasty ass house?"

"What's this," Tyrone smiles from the side of the bed, "You tryina grow some balls on me now?"

"I am tired, Tyrone," she pulls her pants up and wipes a few more tears away, "I'm here all day every day with nothing to do, and no hope for a better, brighter day. Every *fucking* day is the same for me. And you... you go out, you work, you party, you fuck every whore in the city and come back to me smellin' like everybody's vagina. It's not fair, Tyrone! Damn it, it's not fair. I know I'm not much to look at, but I ain't no dog or a slave that you can just beat and screw on command!"

"No, Denise," he stands up, "that's where you're wrong love. That is exactly what you are to me. Now get your ass over here!"

He snatches her towards the bed and rips her pants down past her knees this time. Tyrone takes off his soiled work pants and tosses them atop the filthy laundry pile and then crawls up in the bed and lies back with his hands behind his head.

"Come on up here Denise and do that thing you do." he smiles a crooked smile.

Denise looks beyond him at the closet on the other side of the bed and shakes her head no.

"No, what you mean no," Tyrone growls, "Bitch, get your ass over here and do like I said!"

"I wasn't..." Denise starts.

Tyrone snatches her in the bed before she can finish her statement. The closet door swings open violently.

"Hell no, Denise, "the man from the closet snatches her away from Tyrone, "I can't take any more of this shit!"

"Who the hell are you?" Tyrone scrambles to cover his naked body.

There standing in front of a crying Denise is a man Tyrone has never seen before in his life. He's smaller than Tyrone but not by much. He's light skinned with short curly hair and fire in his eyes.

"Sit still old man," the stranger aims his gun at Tyrone's

head, "nothing new here. I've seen your old fat ass naked on many occasions."

"What the hell," Ty tries to stand up but gets pushed back down quickly, "What is this? And what the hell do you mean you've seen me naked on many occasions?"

"Every time your fat ass gets home from work early," the man explains, "I have to hide in that closet until after you come in and rape my girlfriend for thirty weak ass seconds and then fall your fat ass to sleep. Then I sneak out."

"Denise," Tyrone looks past the man, "What the hell is he talking about?"

"I'm fucking your wife Tyrone," the man claims, "Did you really think your old fat ass could keep this young, vibrant, beautiful woman happy? Hmm... Is that what you really thought?"

Tyrone looks past him at Denise again.

"Hell no," the man continues, "You knew better. You knew from the moment you met her, she was way too damn good for you. So what did you? You did what all insecure men do when they luck up and meet a woman whose self-esteem is just low enough to be tricked into anything. You lied to her and made her feel like she was less than she is. There are a lot of women out there who ain't shit, but Denise ain't one of em'."

"How the fuck would you know she's my wife you little mother fucker!" Tyrone screams from his fat back.

"No," the man smiles at Tyrone, "See that's where you're wrong Tyrone. She was your wife, but now after I kill your stupid ass and hide your fat ass body behind this house she's going to be my wife. She's been mine emotionally for weeks now anyway."

"No Malcolm," Denise cries, "You can't kill him."

"And why not baby," Malcolm turns to look at her, "He treated you like you were worthless baby."

"Yes he did," she agrees, "But now because of you I'm
starting to know my worth so I don't wanna lose you to prison, or worse. He's not worth it, baby."

"Baby," Tyrone screams, "You just called him baby, in my damn face? You evil conniving bitch, I shoulda known you were fucking around behind my back."

"Yes I was, Tyrone," she admits, "But at least I had the decency to do it behind your back. I'm not as bold as you. I'm leaving you Tyrone..."

"No the hell you're not!" Tyrone jumps up for the bed and lunges for Malcolm's gun.

Malcolm cocks the gun, but not quickly enough.

Tyrone wrestles the gun away from him and then drops it on the floor. Malcolm punches Tyrone in the face twice as the older man reaches down for the gun.

Tyrone picks the gun up and Malcolm grabs hold of it before Tyrone can aim it at him. They continue to struggle for control of the deadly weapon as Denise stands back crying out at the top of her lungs.

BANG!!!! Tyrone and Malcolm both fall to the filthy carpet. The flames from the smoking gun are violent but oddly beautiful. The bright blood is everywhere, and all sound has been sucked out of the bedroom. Denise falls to her knees searching for a prayer, but her brain is incapable of anything at this point. As she sees him stand up from the nasty bloody floor, Denise closes her tearful eyes. She knows exactly what she has to do next.

"DOMESTICATED"

MIRROR MIRROR ON THE WALL

YOU'VE BEEN BEATEN AND CRACKED
BUT NEVER DO FALL
I SHOULD PROBABLY BE RID OF YOU
ONCE AND FOR ALL
BUT YOU ARE THE ONLY MIRROR
IN WHICH MY UGLY BELONGS
LOVE YOURSELF THEY SAY
THAT'S THE ONLY WAY TO FIND LOVE
BUT IF YOU DON'T KNOW LOVE'S FACE
HOW THEN DO YOU JUDGE
SEE I BELIEVED HE BEAT ME
BECAUSE HE LOVED & CARED FOR ME
BUT NOW THAT MY FACE IS BROKEN
NOT EVEN I WOULD BE THERE FOR ME
LEAVING IS THE ONLY CURE
BUT I FEAR THAT HE WOULD FIND ME
WHAT IS THIS THING CALLED LIFE
AND WHY HAS IT BLINDED ME
THERE'S A MAN IN MY CLOSET
BUT THE MONSTER WILL NEVER KNOW
PLANTED IN A DESOLATE PISS STAINED GARDEN
HOW WAS I SUPPOSED TO GROW
I KNEW A MAN WOULD COME ONE DAY
TO FINALLY TRY TO SAVE ME
SO I STAND STRONG WITH A SUBMISSIVE FRONT
CAN'T LET THE MONSTER BREAK ME
IF TWO LIKE MINDS
MESH THEIR LONGING SOULS TOGETHER
A BOND IS CREATED BETWEEN THEM
THAT CAN TRULY OUTLAST FOREVER

Butterscotch Rainbows

"Where is your father?" Melanie asks.

"I don't know Mommy," Jessica replies weakly, "I've been here with you all day."

Melanie forces a smile as her very sick daughter looks on.

"I was just thinking out loud little girl," she tells her, "but how are you feeling?"

"Well, I'm still alive..." Jessica whispers through a snaggletooth grin.

"Yes you are, baby," her mother leans down to kiss her yellow cheeks, "And that's not going to change anytime soon."

"Yes, huh," Jessica tries to sit up, "Mommy, you know Dr.
Franklin said I'm a goner..."

Melanie quickly covers her daughter's mouth.

"Jessica," she says, "Mommy doesn't give a damn what Dr. Franklin said, you're not dying on my watch. I know a much better doctor than him anyway."

Jessica gently removes her mother's hand away from her

mouth.

"Who, mama," she asks, "What doctor is better than Dr. Franklin? What's his name Mama?"

"His name," Melanie says, "is Jesus. And he can fix, and cure anything. So mama doesn't give a damn what your doctor says, or any other doctor for that matter, because the only thing that matters is what Dr. Jesus says..."

"Well I do agree with that Mrs. Bridges." a deep voice startles Melanie from behind. She spins around quickly.

"Dr. Franklin," Melanie's cheeks begin to redden, "I was just telling her..."

"No need to explain, Mrs. Bridges," Dr. Franklin assures her, "I totally agree, King Jesus is in control of all things. All I can do is give you my best diagnosis, but ultimately it's up to this beautiful brave little girl and the Lord above."

Melanie smiles down at her daughter's blushing face.

"Thank you, Dr. Franklin," Melanie says, "You are a really good man. You have been the archetype of a dream doctor for us. You just seem to always be right here, and my daughter and I... as well as my husband, David, all appreciate everything you've done for us."

"Just doing my job Mrs. Bridges..." Dr. Franklin grins.

"Yes, I know," Melanie replies, "But you're just a godsend and a blessing to be around. And you're very handsome, I might add."

Melanie begins to blush again.

"Now Mrs. Bridges," the tall handsome doctor smiles, "If I didn't know any better I'd think you were flirting with me."

"I wouldn't say flirting, Dr. Franklin," she replies, "I'm just being open and honest with you, and if I wasn't happily married... which I am, then maybe I would allow you to classify this as flirting..."

They share a good laugh together.

"Is that so," Dr. Franklin says, "Your husband is an attractive man himself, Mrs. Bridges, and very successful as well… or so I've heard."

"Please call me Melanie," she tells him, "And yeah David owns a couple of fitness gyms here in Orlando, and he's cute. But… he's light skin. I never used to even consider dating light skin guys. All my exes were tall dark and sexy like you."

Melanie looks down at the floor.

"Mama…" Jessica calls out quietly from her hospital bed.

"Yes, baby," Melanie looks back at her daughter's confused face, "Dr. Franklin and I are just teasing each other baby. You know I love your father more than life."

"I'm sure you do," Dr. Franklin reaches in his pocket, "here's my card, if you ever need anything just let me know love."

Melanie looks at the card, and then swiftly slides it in her purse. Dr. Franklin scoots past her to get to Jessica.

"How are you feeling this morning beautiful?" he asks Jessica as he places the end of his cold stethoscope on her chest.

"I'm still alive, Doc." Jessica responds with another sweet but painful smile.

"Jessica Bridges," Dr. Franklin says, "you are the most vibrant and happy eight-year-old I have ever met. You are absolutely refreshing to be around. And you know what…"

"What Doc?" Jessica asks.

"I hope Dr. Jesus proves me wrong too." he admits to her.

"Me too Doc," Jessica agrees, "and you know what Doc…"

"Nope," Dr. Franklin says, "But I bet you're going to tell me."

"You remind me of my daddy," she tells him, "you even smell like him. He always smells like butterscotch, it's his favorite candy."

Dr. Franklin smiles awkwardly at Jessica, and then turns around to look at her smiling mother.

"You got a great kid Mrs. Bridges," he clears his suddenly dry throat, "You and your husband are very lucky to have her. Nurse, get Jessica and Mrs. Bridges something to eat, I'm sure they're starving."

"Yes sir, Dr. Franklin." the nurse replies.

Doc rubs Melanie's shoulder ever so gently and then heads towards the door.

"Thanks Doc." Melanie says as he exits the room.

"Don't mention it love." he replies over his broad left shoulder with a genuine smile.

Then Melanie heads towards the door herself.

"Where are you going mommy?" Jessica asks.

"Mommy needs to use the bathroom." Melanie replies.

"Then why were you leaving the room, there's a bathroom right behind you, mommy?" Jessica reminds her mother.

"Please don't leave me alone," she cries, "You're the only one here. My daddy said he would come and stay with me... and bring me lots of butterscotch, but he didn't, so if you leave then I won't have anybody but Dr. Jesus... and I can't even see him mama."

Jessica puts her face in her hands and begins to cry. Melanie rushes back to her sick eight year olds side.

"Jesus is the only one you need baby," Melanie hugs Jessica tightly, "And you don't have to see him, but just know he always there. And mama will use this bathroom, I won't leave you alone I promise baby."

Melanie makes her way inside the bathroom around the corner from her daughter's hospital bed. After closing and locking the door behind her she sits down on the toilet fully clothed and begins to shed a few tears of her own. Melanie can feel her entire body shaking and can't figure out how to make it stop.

"I'm so damn stupid," Melanie cries to herself, "So blind

and too stupid to even deserve to ever be happy. I'm a joke. I'm my husband's obedient little puppet. I didn't mind at first, I loved being submissive to David. It made me happy to know he was happy. Every second of my day was spent obsessing over how to keep my man satisfied. Lord knows I would die for that man... but it's obvious my life just isn't that important to him anymore. But I keep up the façade... and I wear the mask he handcrafted for me. I'm so sorry Lord, because I have worshiped this man and made him like a god in my life. And to think all of our friends are so jealous of our **perfect** marriage, and I used to not blame them, because the happiness David and I shared felt so real. But now I know there's another woman. Lord... I pray whoever she is... she can keep him happy, because I'm just not good enough to do it myself anymore."

Melanie dries her face and exits the bathroom. Instead of walking back to Jessica's bedside, she walks out of the hospital room door with her head held low.

"Melanie..." he says as he rushes down the hallway in a purple polo sweater and peanut butter brown corduroy pants.

She looks up through teary eyes to find her personal god only a few feet away from her.

"Oh, David..." she cries.

"I'm here Melanie." he gently holds her distraught light brown face in his big yellow hands. As Melanie looks up into her husband's beautiful face she's trying with everything in her to hate him, but she's just not capable of doing so.

"Stop crying," he reaches into his left pocket, "Here..."

David stuffs ten butterscotch candies into Melanie's right front pant pocket.

"Where have you been David?" she pulls away from him wiping her face again.

"It doesn't matter Melanie I'm here now," he says, "How is my daughter?"

"I said, where have you been David," Melanie raises her voice as more tears begin to fall, "Do not ignore my question."

"This is not about us," he replies, "I'm asking you how my daughter is doing..."

"She has terminal brain cancer David," Melanie says, "How the hell do you think she's doing? She's dying, David; and the doctors can't do anything to stop it from spreading."

"I'm sorry." he holds his head down.

Melanie laughs awkwardly as more tears begin to storm her disheveled face.

"You're sorry," she says, "Are you serious right now David? Our daughter is only days, maybe hours from dying at eight years old, and all you can say is you're sorry?"

"I am sorry, but I wasn't talking about *that* Melanie... damn it!" he yells.

"Then what the hell are you talking about David?" she inquires.

"I met someone." he admits.

"Yeah I know," she looks sternly at him through new tears, "You met someone a while ago, I just didn't say anything because I was praying to God it was just a brief fling and that she didn't mean anything to you."

"I thought it was just a fling too," he says, "But I've changed Melanie, I'm not the man you married ten years ago..."

"So you're leaving me... for another woman David?" she asks.

"Don't be silly," he laughs, "I would never leave you for another woman Melanie."

"Don't play with me, David," Melanie bursts into painful awkward laughter, "You scared me... I thought you were really leaving..."

"Yes, I am leaving you Melanie," he tells her, "but not for another woman..."

"What the hell David," she screams in terror, "You're telling me you're gay?"

David doesn't respond as he continues to look into his wife's broken heart through her tear stained eyes.

Dr. Franklin approaches the two of them with a calming smile.

"Please lower your voice, Mrs. Bridges," Dr. Franklin says, "we do have other patients and families on this floor."

She ignores the doctor.

"Answer me, damn it," Melanie slaps David hard across the face, "Are you gay, David? You know what? It's obvious you are... I guess deep down it always has been. So where is he? Where is the little sissy?"

"No need for name calling," Dr. Franklin tells her as he takes her left hand in his, "I've been more than nice to you and your sickly daughter since day one. Now honestly, Mrs. Bridges, would you rather David stay with you and live a lie?"

"Wait," she says, "Doc, *you're the one... you've been sleeping with my husband*!"

"No, Mrs. Bridges," Dr. Franklin replies, "that's where you're wrong. You see, David chose me... so *you've* been sleeping with *my man*."

"Nurse Flowers," Dr. Franklin looks just behind Melanie's head, "here, take my coat and stethoscope, I'm resigning effective immediately. Let's go David. I'm taking you on a Mediterranean cruise. I bought the tickets a week ago, we leave out tomorrow tonight."

"But baby, I don't have anything to wear on a cruise..." David tells the doctor.

"No worries love," Dr. Franklin replies, "I bought a whole new wardrobe for you. Its waiting for you at my mansion. Oops, I mean *our* mansion, I mean you did help pay for it."

As the two of them walk away, a completely broken and numb Melanie backs slowly into her daughter's hospital room with a pocket full of butterscotch candy, unsure what to say or do next. She knows full well that Jessica is all she has left now.

"Jessica…" Melanie cries out as she turns the corner near her daughter's bed.

There's a new fresh white sheet over the child's face.

"I'm sorry Mrs. Bridges," the nurse standing next to Jessica's bed says, "Jessica is already gone."

"BUTTERSCOTCH RAINBOWS"

A CHILD SHOULD NEVER FEEL HOW I FEEL
FOR A SECOND OR A MINUTE
WHEN MAMA SAID WE CAN BEAT THIS THING
KID I THOUGHT SHE REALLY MEANT IT
WITH A POCKET FULL OF BITTER CANDY
AND MOUTH FULL OF SWEET LIES
MY OLD MAN PAYS NO MIND
TO THE PAIN IN MY MOTHER'S
EYES I NEED HIM TO BE BETTER
MY FATHER HAS TO CHANGE
THIS CANCER IS ENDING ME
MY LIFE HAS REACHED ITS FINAL PAGE
THE DISDAIN MY FATHER'S FACE DISPLAYS
I ALWAYS FIND SO STRANGE
HOW CAN ANY MAN TREAT HIS WIFE AND DAUGHTER
TO SO MUCH
UNREAL PAIN
HE ACTS LIKE HE'S CLUELESS
MY TIME NOW IS NEAR

THE DOCTORS SAY ANY DAY NOW
SO MOM NEEDS HIM HERE
I DIDN'T MEAN TO GET SICK
HONESTLY IT'S NOT MY FAULT
AND EVEN THOUGH I'LL LOSE THIS BATTLE
DON'T DISCOUNT HOW HARD I FOUGHT
SINCE I'LL DIE YOUNG BURY ME IN SATIN
BUT LAY ME DOWN ON A BUTTERSCOTCH RAINBOW
WITH IMPERFECT WINGS
AND A FADING HALO
I'LL STILL FIND MY WAY TO HEAVEN
SURROUNDED BY GOD'S PERFECT GLOW

If you enjoyed this novel you should check out these other *AMAZING* titles by De'Lure

Onyx Cielo: Book 1 -The Tree of Transformation- (Fantasy)
Take My Breath Away: Orlando Nights –RELOADED-
(Realistic Romance/ Drama)
Take My Breath Away 2: When Love Calls (Realistic
Romance/ Drama)
Take My Breath Away 3: Save me from my Past (Realistic
Romance/ Drama)

Passion Absolute –Radicon's Princess- (Realistic Romance/
Drama/Erotica)
De'Lure Shorts & Poems 2 (Poetry/Drama/Short Stories)
He Without Sin (Realistic/Romance/Drama)
The Art of Beauty (Realistic/ Island Romance/ Drama)
Mental Apex -Black Pyramids- (Deep Poetic Perfection)
Kissed (Murder Mystery/Suspense/ Romance)

Available through Infinitypublishing.com, Amazon.com, Barnes&noble.com, and many other retailers. Signed copies can also be ordered directly from the author.

Email: ceom.love@gmail.com
FB: Published De'Lure